THE VALLEY
of the fraser

A true historic narrative from
Surrey's formative years

John Pearson   ⚘   Lorne Pearson

LIBRARY
William Watson Elementary
16450 - 80 Avenue
Surrey, B.C. V4N 0H3

City of Surrey
British Columbia, Canada
2005

Copyright © 2005 by
The City of Surrey. All rights reserved.

No part of this book may be reproduced or transmitted in any form by any means without permission in writing from the publisher, except by a reviewer, who may quote brief passages in a review.

Printed in Canada
Library and Archives Canada Cataloguing in Publication

Pearson, John (1900-1976) and Pearson, Lorne (1933-)
The Valley of the Fraser: A true historic narrative from Surrey's formative years

Includes index.
ISBN 0-9739109-0-9

Fraser River Valley (B.C.) -- History. I. Pearson, Lorne, 1933 - . II. Surrey (B.C.) III. Title.

FC3894.S97P424 2005   971.1'37
   C2005-905640-1

Published by

City of Surrey
Surrey Museum
17710 56A Avenue
Surrey, British Columbia
Canada   V3S 5H8

www.surrey.heritage.ca

This book was begun in the 1960s and reflects a genre of narrative history that brings the era, the people and the story to life. This document does not reflect the written words that actually took place in the story represented. The words and phrases attributed to the characters are fictional and those of John Pearson. The poems, unless otherwise noted, are the work of John Pearson with the one exception of the first stanza incorporated into Chapter V, which was composed by both John Pearson and John Booth.

All attempts to present an accurate historical account have been provided. For additional historical information concerning this era of Surrey's history, please contact the City of Surrey Archives at 604-502-6459.

COVER: The Anderson Family: Eric, Sarah, William Christian, Eric Edwin and Sarah Ann, c. 1890

Courtesy City of Surrey Archives, 170A05

This book is dedicated to the memory of John Pearson and to all the builders of a better life for the people of Surrey, past, present and future.

Our ancestors have given their time, the most precious resource we have, for time is the essence of life and life is the essence of time.

– *Lorne Martin Pearson, July 2005*

Contents

	Figures and Illustrations	i
	Acknowledgements	ii
	Foreword	iii
	Introduction	iv
Chapter I	The Valley of the Fraser	1
Chapter II	Parting Company	5
Chapter III	Land of Milk and Honey	9
Chapter IV	A Sailor Goes Farming	13
Chapter V	Love Springs Eternal	17
Chapter VI	Lovers' Leap	27
Chapter VII	A Journey to Nicomekl	31
Chapter VIII	Brown's Landing Revisited	41
Chapter IX	A Trip to Semiahmoo Settlement	49
Chapter X	Flour and Coal Oil	55
Chapter XI	The Coming of Spring	61
Chapter XII	Incorporation of Surrey Municipality	65
Chapter XIII	Schools in the Forest	73
Chapter XIV	Then Came the Churches	75
Chapter XV	He Found his Missing Rib	77
Chapter XVI	Stark Tragedy in the Forest	79
Chapter XVII	Down to the Sea Again	83
Chapter XVIII	The Last Picnic	89
	Epilogue	93
	Photo Credits	95
	Index	96

Figures and Illustrations

The Anderson Family: Eric, Sarah, William Christian, Eric Edwin, Sarah Ann – c. 1890

Eric Anderson, c. 1872

Sarah McClinton

Schooner, c. 1872

Map: Surrey's historic rivers and trails

Surrey – Langley Road, c. 1875

Pioneer Cabin

Stó:lō Tree Burial

Wells Farm, c. 1895

Reverend and Mrs. Alexander Dunn

Waterfront scene, Halland, Sweden

Murrays' Corners, c. 1890

Home in the West (sketch)

Crown Title (excerpt)

Brownsville Ferry Slip, 1902

Ferry "Surrey" mid-stream loaded with buggies.

Original Fort, Fort Langley in 1894

Hudson Bay Store, 1880

Anderson Cabin, 2005

Semiahmoo Trail Cairn, 1961

Christ Church, September 1884

Reverend Alexander Bell

Teddy Wade Headstone, 1887

The Anderson Family: Eric, Sarah, William Christian, Eric Edwin, Sarah Ann – c. 1890

Anderson Buggy

The Hornby Home

Anderson Children, c. 1903

Eric Anderson, c. 1911

Eric's Funeral Service, July 17th, 1911

Eric, Runney, Ellen and Henry Anderson, c. 1906

Map of B.C. Electric Railway Stations in Surrey

B.C. Electric Tram near Anderson Station

JOHN PEARSON & LORNE PEARSON

Acknowledgements

A writer's best friend is an editor who can convert an ordinary manuscript into enjoyable reading material. Warren Sommer has done that very thing with this book. Warren carefully read and edited the manuscript and I am sincerely thankful for his patience and encouragement.

Much of the material for this book was supplied by Eric and Sarah Anderson's granddaughter Alva Elliott and her daughter Katherine (Cathy) Brohman, to whom I shall be forever grateful.

I would be remiss in my duty if mention was not made of the 2005 City of Surrey Council and the Manager of Heritage Services for their trust in me and belief in the value of this part of Surrey's history, by supporting the publication of this book to coincide with the opening of our city's new Museum.

– *Lorne Martin Pearson, 2005*

Foreword

The title of this book was taken from a letter by "The Father of British Columbia," Governor James Douglas, to the Colonial Office in London, England, dated May 28, 1849. In his report Sir James stated: *"The Valley of The Fraser contains good land and is capable of supporting a large agricultural population, but that is an exception to the general character of the country, which is valuable chiefly for its inexhaustible forest of the finest timber in the world; and its valuable fisheries which will become a source of boundless wealth to its inhabitants at some future time."*

INTRODUCTION

The Valley of the Fraser is a true historical novel. John Pearson researched the content of this book for several years, constantly striving for accurate information. Within its covers are a number of poems, which unless otherwise noted, are the work of John Pearson. The one exception is the first poetic stanza incorporated into Chapter V, John Pearson and the late John Booth of New Westminster mutually composed this.

Some readers may detect a ring of familiarity in two of the poems included in this novel; these were originally printed in *Land of the Peace Arch*, John Pearson's first book. They were shown to be highly relevant to this novel and have therefore been included.

The hand-hewn log cabin built by Eric Anderson in 1872 is the oldest standing man-made structure in the City of Surrey. The cabin is preserved as a centrepiece of history, located on the same property as the City of Surrey Museum in Cloverdale.

Eric Anderson was born on February 14th 1852 in Halland, Sweden. Halland is approximately 160 kilometres west of Stockholm. Eric was four years old when his father drowned, leaving a wife, an eight-year old daughter and Eric to exist on their own during difficult times.

ERIC ANDERSON
C. 1872

When Eric was eleven, his mother placed him on a British whaling ship for passage to either England or Scotland. Rather than land in Britain, Eric decided to remain aboard that ship, and later served aboard two others, all under the command of the same captain.

In 1872, when Eric was twenty years old, the ship he was on anchored in what was later to become Vancouver harbour. It is at this time that the events described in *The Valley of The Fraser* begin.

SARAH MCCLINTON

Sarah McClinton was a beautiful young widow who was to meet Eric at the Wells farm (Edenbank) in Chilliwack in 1872. Sarah arrived in Fort Victoria two years prior to Eric's arrival in Burrard Inlet. She had two children; a daughter Mary Jane, aged thirteen, and a son, Robert, aged eleven. Neither had travelled with Sarah to the West Coast. Eventually the children came to Surrey to live with their mother and stepfather, Eric.

Sarah was born Sarah Morrison, in Enniskillen County, Ireland, July 30th 1845. On February 16th 1865, she married David McClinton of Bentwick, Ireland. His premature death in 1869 signalled the beginning of difficult times for Sarah, which resulted in her eventual travel to the Wells farm in Chilliwack.

The Valley Of the Fraser

CHAPTER I

As the sun was setting beyond Texada Island, a battered old schooner slowly drifted into the narrow inlet. To the port side, majestic mountains rose, almost perpendicular to the water's edge, until the peaks were obscured in the sky, while on the starboard side, a delta covered by primeval rain forest, unfolded before the sailor's eyes.

Eric Anderson had sailed the seven seas for many years. He revelled in the beauty of Mediterranean shores and the romance of the Gold Coast and saw the moonrise over tropical Pacific Islands, but never before had he witnessed a greater display of natural splendour than this enchanting inlet.

As he watched the dying sunrays paint the mountains in blazing colours, it seemed to him that he had seen this brilliant panorama before. But it could not be so, for he had never sailed this far north on the Pacific.

He then remembered once seeing some paintings from British North America by Paul Kane in the art galleries of London. This indeed must be the inlet that the first European artist on the Pacific Coast had so masterfully interpreted on his canvases.

Eric was so absorbed by the beauty of the inlet that he became oblivious to the activities around him, until the sharp command of Captain Bergh snapped him out of his daydream. While most of the sailors stood in silent awe before the unfolding scenery, Captain Bergh remained unmoved by this tranquil fjord.

For many years, Eric and his fellow sailors had endured the distemper of this heartless sea wolf, which even at its best had been a living Hell. This last trip from the Sandwich Islands had seen the old man's temper perking at a permanent boil and by the time the ship had reached Burrard Inlet; the crew was openly talking of mutiny. It did not seem possible to take any more of Captain Bergh's vexations.

About a mile up the inlet the captain ordered the anchor dropped and the ship made ready for the night. A watch had to be maintained, as the crew did not know what danger might be hidden in the dense forest along the shore. They had earlier seen smoke rising from a bluff at the entrance to the inlet, and felt they had to be prepared for any eventuality.

SCHOONER
C. 1872

Early the next morning, Eric and two companions were given a day's rations, guns and axes, and then sent ashore to cut some special timber for repairs to the ship. Not knowing what danger might await them in the forest, the Captain advised that a lookout would be kept from the ship and that a gun would be fired on the hour. If any suspicious activities were noticed, two shots would be fired as a signal to return to the ship.

Eric and his partners stepped ashore among trees larger than any they had ever seen and set to work falling a suitable fir. They had already decided to desert the ship and as soon as the tree hit the ground they started out through the underbrush and did not even hear the first shot fired from the ship. After walking a full day and all night they came out to a clearing overlooking a large river. In the foreground stood a Native village, and beyond it, a white man's city sloped toward the river's bank. From there, a fertile valley stretched into the distance, culminating in a mountain chain perhaps a hundred miles away. Now Eric knew he had come to the Valley of the Fraser. It was here that he would settle and wrest a home from the wilderness. The sea had given him nothing but hardship; the virgin forest would surely be no more difficult.

Hungry and tired, the three sailors stood looking over New Westminster – the Royal City. The trio did not venture closer for fear that their whereabouts would be reported to any pursuing party from the ship. Keeping to the outskirts of the city, the sailors came to the North Arm of the Fraser River. It was late spring 1872, and the river was now in flood stage. Seeing a Native leisurely drifting by in a large canoe, the sailors hailed him ashore, and offered him a plug of tobacco to persuade him to transport them across the river.

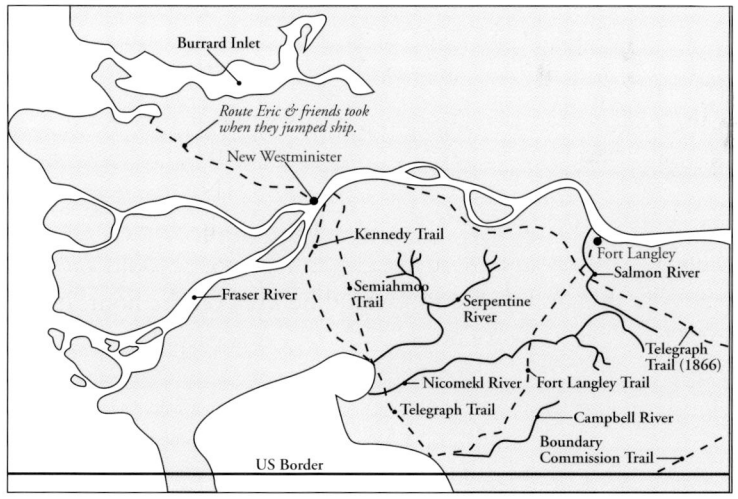

MAP
Surrey's historic rivers and trails

The sailors stepped onto a sandbar where explorer Simon Fraser, some 64 years earlier had met the Natives of this area of the valley that now bears his name. Here too, they found a Native village of some magnitude with several buildings which appeared to been built by Europeans. Their passing through the village did not seem to cause any particular curiosity among the Natives. Nevertheless, they were thankful to come upon a well-beaten trail leading southward as they were fearful of being overtaken by a search party from the ship. Exhausted and hungry, they travelled the whole day and at nightfall stumbled onto an old vacant cabin on the Mud Bay Flats.

Parting Company

CHAPTER II

The cabin was unlike any Native hut they had seen along the way and bore signs of having been occupied by Europeans. The party decided to stop at the cabin for some sorely needed rest. As soon as the men entered the gloomy cabin a gruesome sight threatened to rob them of their newfound haven. What appeared to be a human body was hanging from the rafters, but after closer investigation it proved only to be a sack of mouldy flour.

This was "manna from heaven" for the starving men. Without further delay they mixed some dough and cooked it on a piece of tin that covered the fire pit. With the pangs of hunger stilled, they went to sleep and did not wake until it was nearly dark the following evening. By then it was too late to venture into the unknown forest, so they cooked some more dough and settled down for another night.

The men rose early the next morning and decided it would be safer to split up, as they still feared that a party from the ship would catch up with them. One continued travelling east and was never heard of again, while Albert Anderson headed up the valley and became one of the early settlers of Port Kells.

Eric followed the Nicomekl River upstream until he came to an opening in the forest that he decided to claim as his 'home.'

It was over eight years since Eric had known a home on land; eight years during which he had endured the hardship of the seven seas and abuse from one of the cruellest men to ever wear a captain's cap. Here in God's wonderland he was free – free as the birds twittering in the willows and the trout frolicking in the silvery creek entering the river at his clearing. Little did it matter that hunger was gnawing at him or that darkness was descending over his new home. He was free and in the morning he would find food somewhere, somehow. Exhausted from the ordeal of the past three days, Eric fell asleep in the shelter of a large windfall. In his dreams he was carried back to his childhood and the loving care of a dear mother on a very distant shore.

Sunrays playing on his face woke him the next morning, and as he sat up he had the sensation that someone was watching him. He looked around and was about to dismiss the premonition when he spotted a dusky face peering at him from behind a willow bush. He instinctively reached for his gun, but just as quickly put it down and motioned for the observer to come forward.

The Native walked toward him without any visible fear. He quickly learned that there were others in the bush, and that a hostile move on his part would have quickly spelled the end to his life in the Valley of the Fraser. It was a pleasant surprise to Eric when the Native spoke to him in English. It was as if the primeval forest interpreted itself to him in a language he could understand.

When Eric asked where he could get some food, the Native motioned for him to follow and led the way through the bush for a short distance to another clearing, where several tents made from animal skins stood. Here Eric was given dried fish and some bread made from berries and cornmeal. There were several families living in this camp and Eric learned that they were here to gather berries from the forest and sea trout from the river, and that they would later return to their permanent homes on the coast. The Natives told him of a European settlement farther up the river, where it was possible to buy food and other necessities. Eric had some money although he had forfeited most of his pay when he jumped ship. News of the store within a short distance was more than he had hoped for.

As he started out along the riverbank he came upon a well-beaten trail, and in less than two hours reached a good sized settlement holding a roadhouse, a store and a blacksmith's shop. Eric had arrived at Murrays' Corners, named for the first European to settle there in the early 1870s. Eric wanted to find out all he could about this vast land from people with several years experience as settlers, so he stayed overnight and early the next morning started out for his clearing on the Nicomekl, loaded down with food and tools to begin the long struggle to wrest a home from the wilderness.

SURREY – LANGLEY ROAD
C. 1875

Eric's first concern was to build a lean-to shelter to provide some measure of comfort during the longer and more tedious work of erecting a log cabin. From the settlers at Murrays' Corners he learned that cedar trees were most suitable for building material as this wood was generally straight grained and could be cut and split for any type of construction.

THE VALLEY OF THE FRASER

Eric set to work felling a large cedar to obtain wood for a bunk bed, a table and a bench for his lean-to. When the last rays of the fading sun were seeping through the crowns of the stately evergreens, he retired to his bed of cedar boughs and in the still of the evening began to review the adventures of the past five days. He felt no remorse over the momentous step he had taken. He had come to a friendly land, one apparently unmarred by the greed and selfishness he had observed in Europeans he had known elsewhere.

Land of Milk and Honey

CHAPTER III

Eric had already noticed an abundance of practically everything he needed to sustain life. Only this afternoon a large deer had stood watching him from the edge of the clearing, and there were game birds roosting in many trees. From the Natives living along the river he hoped to learn the secret of survival in this great land.

Gradually drifting into dreamland, he was back on the old ship where the ruthless captain was beating him with a whip until his whole body was burning. Now the old man was pressing him toward an opening in the railing and forced him to take the fatal step overboard. He abruptly sat up in his bunk. He realized it was only a dream, a nightmare, but a burning sensation still lingered over his whole body. Eric found himself surrounded by a cloud of mosquitoes – no, they could not be mosquitoes – they were smaller than anything he had ever seen. He lay down again and pulled the blanket close, but those invisible devils seemed to go right through. Eventually the chill of the night rid him of the attackers and he fell into deep and restful sleep.

The next morning Eric was awakened by a commotion outside his lean-to, and when he looked out he saw a number of Natives pulling a fish net across a pool in the creek. He walked over and bade them good morning. He then rolled up his sleeves and showed them the red, inflamed spots that covered almost the whole of his body. On inquiring what kind of insects could have inflicted this, Eric received the answer, "no-see-ums."[1] At first, he thought it was the Natives' way of evading his question but as they continued repeating the word it dawned on him that no-see-ums was their name for these tormentors of both man and beast.

When the Natives pulled in the net and started back to their camp, they motioned for Eric to follow. At the camp they gave him some salve to soothe his burning skin. They also gave him some evil smelling oil and told him to put it on the bedclothes to keep the no-see-ums away. His first reaction to the smell was to rather suffer the agony from the no-see-ums, but when the night came he was only too glad to use the oil. One could become immune to the evil smell, but not to the torture of the tiny, ravenous insects.

PIONEER CABIN
This cabin is typical of the log structures built in the 1870s[2]

As the days passed, Eric toiled with the big cedars and soon he had cut timber enough to start building his cabin. He selected a location on a knoll that he calculated would be above the high water mark of the river. When work became too monotonous and loneliness overwhelmed him, he would walk to Murrays' Corners to visit his fellow settlers or would set out exploring the surrounding district.

On one of these excursions he came to an island in the Nicomekl River where he discovered a cedar plank box containing a human skeleton tied to the branches of a large fir tree. His first thought was that he had stumbled upon a long forgotten murder, but as he looked around he saw several more similar boxes in other trees. The awesome sight intrigued him. Could this be the result of an ambush during the Cariboo Gold Rush days or was it the remains of some tribal feud in the distant past? He meant to find out and on his way back to the clearing he called at the Native camp and told them of his gruesome discovery. The Natives seemed disturbed over what he had seen and were reluctant to tell him anything about it. Still puzzled over the skeletons in the trees[3] he inquired to the settlers at Murrays' Corners and was told that the Natives would bury their dead by placing them in cedar boxes and hoisting them into a tree. What he had seen was probably an ancient burial ground.

STÓ:LŌ TREE BURIALS

THE VALLEY OF THE FRASER

1 "no-see-ums" – words supposedly spoken by American Indians meaning: "you don't see them. " It is a biting midge.

2 This sod roofed cabin was built by Stove York and Hurricane Smith at Nanaimo in 1872. It has recently been restored by the Nanaimo Museum and is located in Bowen Park.

3 Tree burial was practised by pre-settlement Natives along the Fraser River and when the first settlers arrived, they found skeletons in many of the trees along the South Westminster waterfront. This practice was discontinued as settlers developed the land.

A Sailor Goes Farming

CHAPTER IV

With his money almost gone and winter approaching, Eric became concerned about surviving in the wilderness alone. He inquired at Murrays' Corners about the possibility of obtaining work for the winter and was advised that he might find work at Chilliwack, a growing community about 50 miles up the Valley.

It was now the middle of November. Eric had been burning the stumps from his cleared land and was waiting for two large fires to burn down. After the fires burned down he would head for Chilliwack and the hope of a winter job. From his friends at Murrays' Corners he had learned to make fire do the hard work of falling the great trees. They told him to bore a two-inch hole into the centre of a tree and another about two feet higher on an angle to meet the first one. Charcoal made from maple or crab apple trees, could then be pushed into the holes and ignited. The resultant fire would burn the tree from the inside out, but as there was no sure way of telling in which direction a tree would fall, the process sometimes took its toll of life and property.

One Sunday, Eric was cooking something special for his lonely dinner. His friends in the next clearing had left for their winter quarters on the coast and he was alone in his remote clearing. A cracking noise warned him that one of the burning trees was beginning to fall and he ran outside just in time to see the great fir falling straight into his new cabin, reducing it to kindling. Three months of hard work had been destroyed in a few seconds, but at least his life had been spared. He was still young, just turned 21, and there was enough timber around to build thousands of cabins.

Eric spent the night in the lean-to, and after hiding his tools the following morning, he started for Murrays' Corners and eventually to Chilliwack. When he reached Fort Langley[4] he encountered a party of fur traders about to make a journey to Fort Yale and he was glad to join their company. During their long walk up the Valley, the men told Eric about the Cariboo Gold Rush and the thousands of sourdoughs[5] who had travelled up this Brigade Trail some fifteen years earlier.

At nightfall the party came to a Native village with a European style roadhouse, where they spent the night. When they reached Chilliwack, Eric bade his fellow travellers bon voyage and proceeded to the farm of Allen Casey Wells,[6] following the advice of his friends at Murrays' Corners. Mr. Wells looked kindly upon this big, young man and assured him that there was plenty of work for an additional pair of hands on the farm.

Eric liked what he saw of the surrounding country, especially the rolling meadows and the sleek cattle meandering over the velvety carpet of lush, green grass. He admired the substantial farm buildings dotting the knolls in many directions and was enchanted by the majestic mountains, which bordered the Valley on three sides, providing shelter from the northern storms. The Natives called this place "Valley of the White Waters," and had Eric known that the people here would play an important part in his life, he would probably have been overcome with emotion.

At suppertime Eric was invited into the main room of the log house where all sat down at a large dining table. Here, once again, Eric received a pleasant surprise, for seldom, if ever, had he seen a table laden with a greater amount of good food. Mr. Wells sat at the head of the table and when all were seated he called for quiet. Then in a clear, cultured voice, he prayed for the Lord's blessing of the food.

Mr. Wells then introduced Eric to everyone present, who, without exception, welcomed him with a friendly handshake. Finally Mr. Wells called to the maid, just coming through the kitchen door, "Mrs. McClinton, I would like you to meet the new addition to our humble home, Mr. Anderson." Eric rose and turned around to look into the deepest blue eyes he had ever seen and golden hair that reminded him of a glorious sunset. The strong man who had braved the seven seas and battled the mighty cedars became a weakling who had to grab his chair for support. He regained his poise in time to accept the smooth

Wells Farm
c. 1895

hand reaching toward him and was thrilled when a silvery voice spoke out, "Welcome to our valley."

Again Eric sat down to partake of the abundant food, but somehow his appetite had vanished. This did not pass unnoticed by his host who naturally thought Eric would be famished from his long journey over the Brigade trail. All present looked upon Eric as a new link with the outside world and many questions were asked of him. But Eric's mind was no longer on the rolling ocean or the tropical shores of far-off islands. It was right here in this pioneer home where, a few minutes ago, he had experienced a strange and wonderful feeling. As soon as it was convenient, Eric excused himself and retired to the quarters assigned him, where he lay down on a bunk of sweet smelling hay and began to review the events of the day.

4 Fort Langley was a "stopping-off" place for traders and miners travelling into the fields and streams of British Columbia.

5 A prospector or settler living alone: so called because their staple food was sourdough bread. Historians tell us evidence has been found confirming that sourdough may have first been used around 1300 B.C. in Switzerland. In the California, sourdough bread came popular C. 1845-50, when the gold prospectors carried sours in their backpacks, to be used as starters for leavened bread baked in their campsites.

6 Allen Casey Wells was born in Nappanee, Ontario in 1837, the sixth of ten children to Allen and Martha (Casey) Wells. He came west to the gold fields of British Columbia in 1862. In 1865, Allen Casey and family moved from Yale to Chilliwack to manage the farm of Charles Evans. One year later, he purchased District Lot 38, which was a 150-acre block of land west of Chilliwack River through which flowed the Coqualeetza Creek. The Wells farm was named "Eden Bank" in the 1880s.

Love Springs Eternal

CHAPTER V

Eric had come to a friendly settlement inhabited by people who had accepted him as one of their own. He sat at the table with the master himself. How different from his former master whose private quarters he was never allowed to enter and who handed him his ration of hash on a tin plate. Here, too, he experienced love for the first time and it thrilled him to the marrow of his bones. But then, as a shock, came a second thought, "Mrs. McClinton! Mrs. – wasn't that the English title for a married woman? How could he be so foolish – not thinking of that before and preventing his feelings being noticed by a number of people?"

He would sleep, sleep and forget the dream that could not come true, but his daydreams followed him into the slumber of Morpheus. He was back at the clearing on the Nicomekl and his dream girl was coming toward him as he stood by his little log cabin. With a beautiful smile she was nearing him, but as he reached out to embrace her, she vanished into a mist.

He woke the next morning as the first rays of daylight came seeping through the small window into the bunkhouse he was sharing with Frank McBain, a happy-go-lucky Scot about his own age. It was Frank's second year on the farm and it would be up to him to teach the sailor the rudiments of farming. Several inches of snow had fallen during the night and Frank explained that this meant extra work, as the cattle would have to be driven back from the field and fed at the barn. After breakfast the two men saddled the horses, and as Eric had not ridden horseback for many years, he had some difficulty at first.

As they rode toward the pasture they met two neighbours whom Frank introduced as Tom and Bill Shannon. Eric felt drawn toward these big, handsome men who seemed to carry an atmosphere of wholesome integrity and who gave him an impression that their homespun clothes shielded men of the world. When the Shannon brothers rode on, Frank and Eric rounded up the cattle and drove them back to the farm. The snow went away as fast as it had arrived and there was no more before Christmas.

After lunch, Mr. Wells called Eric in to his private room to discuss his future duties. Eric told him about his training as a ship's carpenter and Mr. Wells explained that there was considerable more building to be done to cope with the expansion of the farm and that he hoped Eric would consent to do the work. Eric said he would do what he could, but would also like to help out with the general farm work as he was anxious to learn as much as possible about farming.

The days turned into weeks and the weeks into months, as work on the farm continued in a routine pattern, but somehow life never became monotonous. There were always deviations from the routine in one form or another. Sundays saw most of the people in the settlement assembling at the Wells farm, where Mr. Wells would read the day's sermon from a large Bible. Occasionally there was dancing in part of the Shannons' barn, which had a smooth wooden floor. Here Eric found Mrs. McClinton to be an accomplished dancer and they had many happy moments as Sarah attempted to teach him the Highland Fling.

Eric had overcome his shyness in Sarah's company, but the question about her husband was always on his mind. Was he working somewhere in this valley preparing a home for his beautiful bride or was he toiling in the creeks of the Cariboo for gold which would give them wealth and happiness in coming years? Eric did not know and would not ask anyone. He would continue to subdue his feelings for her until early summer and then return to his clearing on the Nicomekl.

Work kept him busy from daylight to dusk, and left little time to brood over unrequited love. He was glad of Frank's company and all the things he learned from this likeable son of the Highlands. Unlike himself, Frank was brought up on a large farm and knew all the ins and outs of farming, and he never seemed to tire of teaching Eric.

It was now an evening between Christmas and New Year's and as they retired to the bunkhouse, Frank seemed to have lost his usual high spirits. Eric thought he was homesick and longing for the festivities of his childhood Christmases. Eric felt there was not anything he could do to cheer Frank, so he busied himself with his favourite hobby, writing poetry.

From the first day he set foot in British Columbia, Eric had tried to write something about this beautiful west land. A few stanzas had come to life but not any poetic composition:

> *Beautiful land by the ocean, gem of the golden west*
> *Where sunset tints a silver sheen, On Pacific's heaving breast.*

Eric was pleased with the opening lines and the metre seemed to suit. Slowly and painfully he continued to write:

> *Whose waters lap on the rocky shores, Of great and rugged land, Of canyons deep and waterfalls, Where silent forests stand.*

Eric's poetic mind carried him over the western slopes and the words were forming faster than he could write them down:

> *Land of hidden treasure troves, Rich beyond compare,*
> *Lakes like giant mirrors clear, reflecting nature fair.*
> *Mighty rivers, deep and wide, Seaward race and roll,*
> *Bearing precious living wealth, Blessings rich to all.*

He paused for a moment, then continued:

> *This is the garden God did make, and planted in the West.*

A stir from the other end of the bunkhouse interrupted him and he turned around to see Frank looking at him with a curious expression. "Eric," he said, "I must talk to someone and I know you will listen to me with friendly understanding. Two years ago I came up the Fraser on the last steamer before freeze-up, headed for the golden creeks of the Cariboo. In Hope I met hundreds of miners drifting down from the Cariboo to winter on the coast. They advised me to do likewise, as the cold winters in the gold fields made it impossible to do any mining and the cost of living was extremely high. I took their advice and the next morning started walking back to the coast."

"I did not particularly cherish the thought of going back to New Westminster or Victoria, so when I reached this settlement I called upon the Shannon brothers and inquired if work could be obtained here for the winter. Tom Shannon said Mr. Wells had mentioned he was looking for an extra hired man and he took me to his farm, where Mr. Wells promptly gave me a job. I was glad to get winter work as I needed more funds for outfitting to go to the gold fields. But, when spring came something happened that kept me on the farm and now two years later, I am still here."

"On the first river steamer in the spring came Sarah McClinton, and my dream of the Golden Cariboo faded before the radiance of this beautiful woman, I was content with staying forever just to be in her presence. She dominated my thoughts by day and my dreams at night, but not until this day did I have the courage to propose to her. She said she loved me like a brother, but could never think of me as her husband. Her heart belonged to someone else and she would wait until that someone came to her. Well I am glad it is done and as soon as springtime returns to the mountains I am heading for the Cariboo, and perhaps gold, love and fame."

When Frank stopped talking it was Eric's turn to be puzzled. "Frank!" he said, "How could you propose to a married woman? Obviously you could not expect to marry an already married woman even in this wild land."

Frank's reply was swift, "Eric, I thought you knew that Sarah is a widow and very eligible to marry any red blooded bachelor in the Valley of the Fraser."

"Sarah, a widow, free to marry anyone she would fancy." The thought struck Eric like a bolt from the blue. All the love and emotion he had fought so hard to subdue returned a thousand-fold.

Although Frank did not know for sure, he suspected that Eric was the subject of Sarah's affection and he did not fail to tell him so. When Eric finally went to bed, a peaceful calm descended over his troubled soul. At breakfast the next morning Sarah seemed more radiant than ever and she seemed to have a special smile for Eric.

Day after day the dreary winter slipped by, but the continual work of keeping things going prevented their lives from becoming monotonous. In the middle of February there came a silver-thaw; everything turned to ice and nature went to sleep. One morning Eric noticed hundreds of small birds frozen solid, still clinging to the branches of alder trees around the barn and he could not imagine the fate of any other wildlife caught in this freak ice storm.

Eventually everything comes to an end, and so it was that the latter part of March saw a final end to this hard winter of 1873. The cattle were again in the pasture, but the lush green carpet had turned to a dirty brown colour from being pressed so tightly to the ground over the winter and it was difficult for the cattle to forage sufficient food. There was still a large haystack along the river so the cattle had to be driven to the riverbank to save hand feeding at the barn.

In the beginning of June, Frank spoke to Mr. Wells about his intention of leaving for the Cariboo. Mr. Wells was very sorry to see him go, knowing he would be hard to replace, but this shrewd gentleman fully understood the reason for Frank quitting and did not wish to place any obstacles in his way. He paid his outstanding wages, which gave Frank the assurance of a good grubstake for the gold fields.

After Frank was gone a gloom descended over the people on the farm. Perhaps none realized how much this cheerful Scot had contributed to everyone's happiness. He would long be missed by the people of the settlement.

It was Mr. Wells' practice to give his help Sunday afternoons off whenever possible and now, as nature unfolded its beauty in the spring and summer, Eric and Sarah spent many happy afternoons and evenings strolling over the countryside. There were a number of Native villages in the district and Natives were frequently employed as extra help on the farm. Both Eric and Sarah liked the Native people, who often surprised them with their adaptation to changes in the Valley.

Many of the young Natives appeared to be well educated in European ways, though to Eric, they seemed less inclined to agriculture. They would follow the salmon run up the Fraser in the fall, processing great quantities of dried fish. Some of them told Eric how the narrow canyon above Yale was like Nature's smokehouse. The prevailing winds through the canyon would cure fish better than any other known method. This reminded Eric about the ancient King Solomon and blast furnaces, which Eric heard of while sailing the Mediterranean. Solomon's furnaces were also designed to take advantage of the prevailing winds.

A few of the Natives had small farms of their own with some cattle, but in most cases the stock was left to forage in the bush with rather disappointing results. Many times during the winter, Native mothers came to the farm with ailing children. The babies could not sustain health on dried fish and venison, so Mrs. Wells gave the mothers vegetables and milk to nurses their children back to health.

On a Sunday late in June, Eric asked Mr. Wells if he and Sarah could visit the Coqualeetza Native Mission at Sardis. Mr. Wells agreed and let them have a pair of saddle ponies, as the distance was a little too far to travel on foot. Both Eric and Sarah had heard much about this Mission, but when it came into view they could hardly believe their eyes. The place was like a rambling city encircled by a beautiful stream and in the centre rose a mansion unlike anything they had seen in this new land.

They rode up to what appeared to be the main entrance and even before they dismounted two neatly dressed Native boys approached to take care of their horses. Another boy came over and told them that the Sunday service was about to begin and said he was instructed by the Minister to invite them to attend. They were led into an appealing chapel already filled with people, mostly Natives, but also some European settlers.

It had been many years since either Eric or Sarah had seen the inside of a chapel the sermon was delivered by the venerable Dr. Dunn, who was a visiting guest Minister at the church. Reverend Dunn left a deep impression upon them. After the service they were invited into the study by Reverend Dunn, where they also met a number of the Mission teachers. There they learned of the tremendous task of bringing Christianity and education to people who were still practicing to the customs and beliefs of their ancestors.

REVEREND AND MRS DUNN

Eric was particularly impressed with what he heard, because he had noticed many European settlements without any organized effort to teach their children the three Rs. If this trend continued, he thought, the Natives would be the future elite and the Europeans the drawers of water and hewers of wood.

After informal conversations with teaching staff, Eric and Sarah were invited to join them at dinner, an occasion they would long remember.

Eric had decided to ask Sarah a vital question on the way home, but now they rode in silence as the evening shadows swept over the ancient Native trail. They were both overwhelmed by emotion and memories from childhood days, brought forward by the visit to the Mission. They understood and respected each other's feelings, which left no room for idle talk.

Eric thought of his mother, who perhaps at this very moment was sitting alone thinking of him, or maybe kneeling in the little chapel on the hill praying for his well being. He thought fondly of her, the only woman who ever meant anything to him until met Sarah. Then he thought of the great poet who wrote so beautifully about a mother's love, and he tried to translate into English, the touching stanza:

> *Where is a love that never falters,*
> *Throughout life and eternity?*
> *In this world there is only one,*
> *A mother's love for her only son.*

It was late when they reached the farm and with a rather abrupt good night to Sarah, Eric retired to the bunkhouse, where he sat down to take stock of the situation. What was coming over him? By now he should be down at his clearing beside the Nicomekl, rebuilding his cabin and clearing the land. He longed for his "home" in the wilderness where he could be his own boss, but without Sarah, his dreamland on the Pacific would be bleak and dreary, yes, even meaningless. He would do like Frank; stay until he had enough courage to ask for her hand.

The summer passed quickly. They were already into the harvest season. A number of Natives were employed to dig potatoes and to help with haying. With Eric as foreman, things were operating smoothly.

Eric had little chance to enjoy Sarah's company as she was regularly needed in the kitchen to help prepare meals for the large crew. Mr. Wells was quite aware that Eric and Sarah were pining for an evening on their own, so on a Sunday late in August, he suggested they saddle up two ponies and go for a ride.

Lovers' Leap

CHAPTER VI

The couple rode east on the Brigade Trail until they came to a sheer bluff rising several hundred feet above it. Sarah challenged Eric to race to the top and he accepted with a smile, dismounted, and hobbled the ponies. They circled to the back of the bluff where the ascent was quite easy, but the race was soon forgotten when Eric had to help Sarah over windfalls and other obstacles. Reaching the top they were confronted with a view so breathtaking that they stood in silent awe.

They were standing in a vortex formed by majestic mountains on three sides, looking down the Valley of the Fraser, to where it lost itself in the Pacific Ocean. It was Sarah who broke the spell by telling Eric that this bluff was called Lovers' Leap and was steeped in Indian lore and legend, "A long, long time ago, a young brave from the Slallaham Tribe in the Fraser Canyon started down the river in his dugout canoe to see the big waters of the setting sun. He stopped at the village of The White Waters to visit some kinsmen living there and fell in love with a beautiful princess."

"When word reached the Chief that his daughter wanted to marry a commoner from an inferior tribe, he became very angry, and as a result of this, the young couple attempted to elope up the Fraser Canyon. They struck out through the great timber and had reached the foot of this bluff when they heard pursuers approaching. In a frantic attempt to evade them, they headed for the top of this bluff. The pursuers passed the bluff but returned when they failed to find the tracks of the young couple continuing, and soon came charging up the slopes. The princess and her brave were standing on this very spot and when the war party was within a short distance, the couple joined hands and leaped into eternity. And that is the story of how this cliff got its name."

Eric had listened to Sarah's narration of the Native legend with an amused smile, but now he became serious and said in a stammering voice, "Sarah! If you don't promise to marry me this minute, I feel I shall be following your lovers of yore." Sarah gave him a radiant smile and exclaimed, "Oh! You big, handsome Swede, I had almost given up hope that you would propose to me. Of course I will marry you, and I have a premonition that our love will be as true as those lovers of long ago who chose death before life divided." They embraced and their lips met in a seal of eternal love.

As they sat down on a rock ledge, Eric began telling her about the clearing on the Nicomekl that he called his home; the deep, black soil that would grow anything; the Pacific Ocean, whose breakers could be heard on a stormy night; and the warm Japanese currents lapping on the coast, creating a temperate climate.

As they stood up ready to leave this lofty place, Eric swung Sarah around for a final look down the Valley of the Fraser. He pointed to where the end of the valley met the ocean and said that there, surrounded by stately evergreens, was their home on the Pacific. When Eric stopped talking, Sarah snuggled up to him and said, " I too, love 'Our Home' on the Nicomekl."

As soon as they returned to the farm Eric and Sarah called on the Wells to announce their engagement. Both Mr. And Mrs.

Wells appeared pleased by the news and at supper Mr. Wells announced their engagement to the staff.

Everyone seemed pleased and the women's first concern was for the wedding, but no date could be set due to the uncertainty of a minister being available. The men, on the other hand, discussed the physical problems. It was too late to return to the Nicomekl before winter set in, so Eric agreed to stay on the farm until the following summer. This met approval of the Wells, who were pleased at having Eric and Sarah for at least another few months.

Early December saw the arrival of Reverend Alexander Dunn, who had travelled by horseback to Chilliwack. Eric and Sarah's marriage took place on December 17th 1879, and was one of the first Christian weddings solemnized in the Land of the White Waters. The only change brought about by this historic wedding was that Eric moved from the bunkhouse into Sarah's comfortable chamber in the big log house.

Another winter, not so hard as the first, went by and Eric asked for three months off to go down and do some building at his place on the Nicomekl. He arrived at Murrays' Corners, some four miles from his place, to find the settlement had almost doubled in size during his brief absence. The Murrays were glad to hear that Eric had found a mate for life and welcomed the prospect of having a married couple for neighbours. So many homesteaders were bachelors who succumbed to the loneliness and monotony of the forest and left their clearings in despair.

When Eric reached his clearing he found his tools where he had left them and the lean-to still liveable. He set to work rebuilding his splintered log cabin and later built a lean-to barn, working from daylight until dusk and only stopping long enough to wipe the sweat from his brow. Eric stood six feet five inches and was built like a Nordic god, so he could endure the physical exertion without difficulty.

Whenever he paused for a moment, he could hear the sound of falling trees in many directions and was glad to hear that other Europeans were settling in the district. Who were they and what prompted them to tackle the superhuman job of taming this wilderness? Were they men like him, driven by an incentive of creating a home for a beautiful bride, or bachelors struggling to get a place of their own? He did not know, and he could not now spare the time to find out. On one of the first days in August he stopped to take stock of his work, and often said in later years, "No one worked harder and faster than I did during those three months, nor did the chips fly more furiously."

When he started back to Chilliwack in the fall, he was pleasantly surprised to see work crews building a wagon road, replacing the Hudson's Bay Company's old Brigade Trail.

At the farm, he found Mr. Wells shorthanded as most of the Natives had gone up the river fishing and many of the other labourers had taken employment on construction of the Yale Wagon Road. Many new people were coming into the valley. The road builders regularly called at the farm for supplies and the place had the appearance of a general store.

Eric and Sarah decided to remain on the farm until the Yale Wagon Road was finished so they could make the move in a wagon. When the wagon road was passable they started out for their future home on the Nicomekl. Eric bought a mare in foal for next to nothing and Mr. Wells threw in an old farm wagon, a milk cow and her one month old heifer.

Eric and Sarah acquired every kind of seed used in the valley, three sacks of potatoes and other vegetables, six laying hens with a rooster, two dozen hatching eggs, six duck eggs and a sow which produced seven piglets six weeks later. In addition, the couple loaded tools, bedding, ammunition and a stove into the wagon, which by now began to resemble Noah's Ark. They had everything with which to start housekeeping, including several large pieces of canvas that Eric often said were priceless.

A Journey
To Nicomekl

CHAPTER VII

The couple started down the wagon road with Sarah and the calf riding in the front of the wagon, the pig in the back and the cow forming the rear guard. It was a slow and tedious journey as they could only make ten to twelve miles a day. Toward evening of the first day they came to a Native village at the foot of Sumas Mountain, and were directed to an old barn where they made themselves quite comfortable for the night.

As this was early spring, very few salmon had ventured up the Fraser River. The people of Sumas Mountain were depending on what fish they could catch in the lake for their existence. Eric noticed that they had a good supply of ducks and other waterfowl. When Eric inquired how they caught them, he was told they used nets. He could not understand how ducks could be caught in nets. On their way along Sumas Lake the following morning, he was to see the nets in operation.

In his dealings with the Natives at Chilliwack, Eric was impressed by their pleasing simplicity, personal kindness, innocence, and their scrupulous honesty. It did much to draw him toward these aboriginal people. Now, as they were sitting around a campfire, at the foot of Sumas Mountain, fighting clouds of mosquitoes, Chief Sketkalein of the Sema:th (Sumas) told of two settlements[7] west of Sema:th Lake, with hotels and stores where one could buy anything if you had money. Both Eric and Sarah had saved most of their wages at the Wells farm, and since there were so many things they needed for starting housekeeping of their own, they decided to visit these places the next day.

After bidding their newly made friends farewell, they had only travelled a short distance when they came to a large net suspended high above the ground between two trees. It appeared to be about fifteen feet in depth and was raised or lowered by ropes and wooden pulleys. There were several ducks struggling in the net and it seemed to Eric and Sarah a cruel method of trapping the birds, but they supposed the Natives would be along shortly to end their suffering. Eric and Sarah reached Sumas City early in the afternoon and left their animals in a livery stable then took a room in the Hotel Mt. Baker.

It was a wonderful relief to be rid of the mosquitoes for a while. Since starting out from Chilliwack they had been continuously tormented by clouds of insects so thick that when they tried to brush them off, the motion of their hands drew others in. Eric was told that a number of settlers had pre-empted land as early as the 1860s on the fertile land along the lake, but never really lived on their properties for long, if at all, having been driven off by the mosquitoes. People could shield themselves with netting, but there was no protection for the cattle and many succumbed through loss of blood and infection. In Sumas City, resourceful pioneer women were wrapping paper around their legs under their stockings as a protection against the insects' stings. Eric thought that was a good idea and suggested Sarah try it, as by now her shapely legs were very swollen and painful looking.

After a brief rest at the hotel, the couple walked around Sumas City and were surprised to find three stores and two hotels at this outpost in the developing Northwest. Sarah bought some cloth and a few household things and Eric purchased a good supply of ammunition for the rifle he constantly carried for their protection. They could have bought many other things they needed, but the farm wagon was already overloaded. The couple accordingly decided to wait and to make a trip to New Westminster after they were settled on the Nicomekl.

Early the next morning, Eric and Sarah returned to the livery stable and made ready for another day's journey. They had hopes to reach Shortreed's Corners[8] before nightfall of the third day, but two or three miles from the settlement a large windfall across the road blocked their progress. In surveying the situation, Eric found that a heavy stand of timber prevented him from driving the wagon around the windfall. To cut through the seven-foot fir would take several hours. The tree had embedded itself into the ground. Even if Eric were to cut out a section large enough to drive the wagon through, he would not be able to roll the section of fir out of the trough. The alternative was to take the wagon apart and pass or skid it over the windfall, but Eric and Sarah would not be able to do that in the short time of remaining daylight, so they decided to camp by the fallen tree for the night.

Together, the couple built an improvised lean-to in the shelter of the windfall and Eric began sliding the provisions and wagon parts over the log. Sarah busied herself making the camp comfortable and started to prepare the evening meal. As dusk descended over the wilderness, they sat down to a wholesome meal and made light-hearted jokes about their misfortune. Little did it matter that they were delayed a day on the journey to their new home; they were young, healthy and happy, with a full life unfolding before them. They had both known privation and want in an old world, but here in this beautiful west land they were free from ancient tradition and physical needs, free to mould their own lives and future.

In the shimmering twilight they reclined on a bed of cedar boughs and lay watching the stars twinkle through a crown of stately evergreens. There had been so little time for talk at the busy Chilliwack farm and now Sarah began to ask Eric about his home and childhood. She learned that he had been born in Halland, west of Stockholm near the coast of Sweden, and that his forefathers had been sailors for many generations. His grandfather had been lost at sea before Eric was born and his father met the same fate when Eric was just four years old. With the loss of his father, life became a struggle both for Eric and his mother. Many times they experienced near starvation and other severe hardships.

WATERFRONT SCENE
Halland, Sweden

When he was eleven, Eric's mother placed him on a whaler with intentions that he would be dropped off in either Scotland or England. However, from that time on, he had sailed on various ships, always under the same heartless captain. As Sarah listened to him, a knowing feeling came over her, a fear that some day, the call of the sea would be so strong that Eric would return to the profession of his ancestors. But he assured her that he would never leave this enchanting valley or her. Together, they would remain and build a new home for themselves and for generations yet unborn.

Now it was Eric's turn to ask Sarah about her early years on the Irish Coast. There was always a question on his mind, which he dared not ask:

Did she still love the young man she had married when she was not much more than a child, did her heart still pain over him being swallowed by the cruel sea after only a brief time of wedded harmony?

These questions drifted through his mind like a shadow, he did not know why, he certainly had no reason to doubt the love of this woman who had pledged to be his until "death do us part."

Then Sarah began telling him her childhood memories. Her family was poor and many times lacked even the barest necessities of life. Their mainstay was fishing supplemented by whatever they could eke out of the barren ground. At the age of nineteen, on February 16th 1865, she had married David McClinton. Sarah and David had known each other since childhood, and she did not feel much different toward David than toward some of the other young men in the village. Somehow it had seemed a foregone conclusion they would marry as soon as they came of age. They were married less than four years when David died. His death left her lonelier than ever on the bleak and barren coast, and she began dreaming about the outside world.

Sarah had many hard times ahead. She went back to her parents' home, but a short while later her father died and the family dispersed and travelled throughout the world. Sarah and her brother Robert travelled to British Columbia. An uncle of her late husband had travelled to West Coast of British North America a few years earlier, so she had written him telling of David's tragic death and her longing to leave for some other part of the world. Robert McClinton invited his niece to come to British Columbia. When she arrived at Fort Victoria, there was a message for her from her uncle to take a river steamer to Chilliwack and report to the Wells farm. She sent word from Victoria to Chilliwack and when she arrived there he met her.

Mrs. Wells needed help on the ever growing farm and Mr. McClinton was better pleased with Sarah there than residing in his rowdy roadhouse in the Fraser Canyon. She had been on the Wells' farm two years when Eric arrived and she thought he knew pretty well every move she had made since.

When Sarah stopped talking, the last shadow of doubt cleared from Eric's mind, he knew then that her love for him was as true as she was beautiful.

It was still early and the spring air became quite nippy as the evening drew on. The pair had been lying slightly apart under the single blanket but now Sarah cuddled up to Eric and in a caressing embrace they drank the sweet nectar of nature. Theirs was a happy and carefree life, the privation and want they had known from their childhoods was receding before the friendliness and abundance of this paradise on the Pacific Northwest Coast.

They were awakened the following morning by the clatter from a woodpecker attacking the windfall for some delicious breakfast. Well, it was time to get up anyway. They had chores to attend to before continuing the journey; the cow had to be milked, the calf, the pig and chickens fed and a hearty breakfast must be prepared for themselves so they could continue through the day without delay.

After a couple of hours of travel they reached Shortreed's Corners. They stopped only long enough to exchange greetings and dispose of some surplus milk and eggs. Later in the day when they met a stagecoach heading for the Cariboo, Eric told the driver about the large windfall blocking the road. The driver said it was common occurrence and they were well equipped to undertake the necessary work.

Eric and Sarah continued their slow journey for three more days without further delay, reaching Murrays' Corners, where they stopped overnight. Mrs. Murray took an instant liking to Sarah, who in turn thought a lot of this jolly woman with an air of a matron about her. The two women were mutually happy at the prospect of being neighbours in the future.

Murrays' Corners
c. 1890

The next morning, Eric and Sarah set out over the newly constructed McLellan Road, which took them to the Shannon homestead at Clover Valley. Thomas and William Shannon had left Chilliwack the previous summer and had resettled on nine hundred and forty acres along McLellan Road. They would now be Eric and Sarah's closest neighbours in this new settlement. William Shannon named the area Clover Valley, but when the first railway was built through the district in 1891, the engineers changed the name to Cloverdale.

Eric and Sarah had become very fond of the Shannons at Chilliwack and were naturally happy to see them settle so close to their homestead. In their opinion, the Shannons were genuine, fearless men, the kind needed to form the backbone of this new country.

As nothing more than a blazed trail led to their homestead on the Nicomekl, the farm wagon had to be unloaded at the Shannon homestead. After lunch Eric asked Sarah along for a walk to see their future home. When the homestead came into view,

Eric stepped aside and motioned for Sarah to walk ahead. He was anxious to see if Sarah would approve of his choice of their future home. She stopped and silently admired the beauty of the river and the sparkling creek, which entered at the edge of the clearing. Then her gaze caught the good-sized log cabin, a barn and two outbuildings. Below them stretched a meadow covered with a luxuriant green carpet. When she finally turned around to face Eric, it was with tears in her eyes, tears of happiness. She came up to him and pressed her lips to his with a gratifying and approving kiss. Eric felt as if this was a seal of assurance for a long happy life.

HOME IN THE WEST
How the Anderson farm may have looked when Sarah first saw it.

The couple were standing on the delta of the Fraser. A few acres of its five millions were to be their own to till and toil as best they knew. It did not worry them that in this immense wilderness there were only a handful of homesteaders, or that behind the large evergreens there might lurk unknown dangers. Fear and loneliness would never overwhelm them, for love and companionship would carry them through trouble and tribulation.

As they walked up to the buildings and began inspecting everything, Sarah was amazed by all the work Eric had accomplished during the three short months the previous summer and she thought he must be the best husband in the entire Valley. The cabin had a solid door split from a cedar log, a table made from the same tree and two stools fashioned from half round logs. A partition divided the cabin into two rooms that she thought to be a kitchen and a bedroom. In the bedroom she found a six-foot bench and a good-sized bed made from cedar slats. With a gleam in her eyes she viewed the primitive bedstead, perhaps thinking how nice it would look draped with the multi-coloured quilt she had made during the past winter in Chilliwack.

In her childhood Sarah had slept on a mattress of eiderdown. Eric said he was sorry; she would have to be content with sleeping on hay until the fall when he would gather the soft, downy tops from bulrushes, which were the pioneers' substitute for eiderdown.

As they walked back to Shannons' homestead, Eric was contemplating the best way to freight their goods through the bush. He was at a loss to figure out how to move the heavy kitchen stove to the homestead, until he remembered seeing the Natives using two poles tied to the back of a horse with the ends trailing on the ground. He believed they called the contraption a travois. He mentioned the idea to Tom Shannon, who said he thought he had some suitable poles. In a few minutes they had the travois attached to a harness on the mare and Eric was on his way with the kitchen stove. It amazed him how easily the travois seemed to ride over bumps, stumps, and windfalls. Anywhere the horse could go, the travois followed.

On the second day at their property, Sarah remained at the homestead while Eric returned for the balance of their goods. He was reluctant to leave her alone, even for an hour or so, for he had heard stories about settlers being accosted by tramps or hoboes. There were also bear and other predators that might attack humans under certain circumstances, so he left his rifle with her. He impressed upon her to have the gun ready at all times and not to hesitate using it, always keeping in mind that the law prevailing here was law of the wilderness: "to kill or be killed."

By the time Eric returned, it was quite late when they sat down to their first dinner in their new home. After dinner, Sarah related she liked to listen to the distant roar of the breakers rolling along the coast, but the evening was still and all nature seemed to slumber. The silence of the wilderness became almost overwhelming and they retired their first night in the cedar bunk. The physical exertion of a long day soon took its toll on the couple, lulling them into a deep and restful sleep – two happy children sleeping peacefully in the vastness of the west land, oblivious to the outside world.

> 7 A Boundary Commission Survey map of 1861 places a survey camp on the north edge of one of the larger bends of the Sumas River, in Washington State, U.S.A., about a mile and one-half south of the International Border. {Sumas City}. On the Canadian side, Huntingdon did not come into existence until 1891. The area had no name prior to that year.

> 8 Shortreed's Corners later became part of what Philip Jackman (reeve of Langley, 1895-97) was to call Alder Grove, because of the abundance of alder trees in the area.

Brown's Landing Revisited

CHAPTER VIII

With the break of day, nature exploded into a deafening crescendo from all directions. It was difficult to distinguish one sound from another since many were new and strange to them. The airy screech of the seagull was a familiar sound to them, as was the drumming of the grouse, but there were some intonations they had not previously heard. Eric and Sarah became fascinated by the display of trout jumping in the little creek. They appeared as an inexhaustible supply of rich and wholesome food. Sarah suggested fish for breakfast, so Eric got his tackle ready and in a few minutes caught two trout for a delicious breakfast in their new home.

Later, Eric advised that he would have to go to New Westminster as soon as possible to purchase a plough. It was important that they get enough land broken and seeded to assure food both for them and for their stock through the coming winter. It was decided that Eric would go the next day, and if he did not make it back before nightfall, Sarah could stay with Mrs. Shannon overnight.

Before starting out, Eric again handed Sarah the gun and asked her to keep a close watch over their homestead. At Shannons', he hitched the mare to the old farm wagon and started out along the McLellan Road. He then came to the Semiahmoo Wagon Road, over which he travelled as a fugitive some years earlier. The old Native trail had now been rebuilt into a wagon road of good quality on which he was able to put his horse to a trot. When he reached Brown's Landing, on the south bank of the Fraser, there appeared to be fewer Natives than when he first saw the area. In their place were quite a few European people.

Eric stabled his horse and was taken across the river in a large canoe, but this time he had to pay cash for the trip, in contrast to the plug of tobacco that had been acceptable payment for his first trip across the Fraser. He thought the Natives had learned well the value of money since he had first had dealings with them.

CROWN TITLE
Excerpt

> To all to whom these presents shall come, Greeting:
>
> **Know ye,** that WE do by these presents, for US, Our heirs and Successors, in consideration of the sum of _____ Dollars, to US paid, give and grant unto _____ his heirs and assigns, All that Parcel or Lot of Land situate in _____ District, said to contain _____ acres, more or less, and more particularly described on the map or plan hereunto annexed and coloured red, and numbered _____ on the Official Plan or Survey of the said _____ District in the Province of British Columbia, to have and to hold the said Parcel or Lot of Land, and all and singular the premises hereby granted, with their appurtenances, unto the said _____

In New Westminster, Eric called at the Land Registry Office to register his pre-emption and then went to the T. G. Trapp general store where he purchased a plough and some other needed things. He had thoughts of getting a lighter gun for Sarah and when Mr. Trapp brought forth a Winchester 74, he included it in his purchase. It did not take him long to finish the shopping and start on his return trip. Eric arrived at the Shannon homestead around dusk and Sarah was there to meet him. She was excited and still shaking from an encounter with a bear earlier in the evening. After putting the cow, calf, and chickens into the barn and the pig into the sty, she had returned to the cabin to finish her chores. The still of the evening had been pierced by a squeal from the pig. Sarah had picked up the gun and ran outside to see a bear tearing away at the pigpen, so she fired the gun with a result that the bruin scurried off into the timber. Sarah did not believe she had hit the bear, but thought that if she had a lighter gun she would be able to take care of anything threatening their stock. Eric listened to her with a sombre look on his face, fully realizing what a blow the loss of the pig would have been to them at this time. Then he reached into the wagon, turned around and handed Sarah the Winchester 74 he had purchased in New Westminster. Sarah took the gun and put it to her shoulder several times; she was as happy with it as a child is with a gift at Christmas.

Eric was concerned about getting back to their homestead as soon as possible. There was no predicting what the bear might do, so they left everything at Shannons' and walked toward home. The bear did not return during the night. Eric was sure it would show up sooner or later, for he had heard bear were particularly ravenous for pigs. In the morning, he suggested that Sarah practice with the new rifle. He blazed some bark from a tree for her and told her to start shooting. She missed the tree entirely on her first two tries. Eric thought the gun's sights might need adjusting so he tried the gun himself. His first shot cut the edge of the blaze and the second was dead centre, so he handed the gun back and told Sarah to keep practicing. She fired several more rounds, still missing the tree. Disappointed, Eric left her to target practice and went about his day's work.

As the days slipped by Eric was ploughing as hard as he dared drive the pregnant mare, and since the rich alluvial soil was quite easy to break, he soon had a good-sized field ready for sowing. Sarah spent a lot of spare time practicing with her new gun, but she would not shoot again in Eric's presence. She was still smarting from his remark that she couldn't hit a barn door. She was secretly planning to get even with him.

One day Eric went to Surrey Centre to borrow a harrow from another settler, Abraham Huck. On his return, Sarah met him at the edge of the clearing. She was carrying her gun and with a broad smile asked Eric to look at the small blazes on the trees, with a bullet hole dead centre in each blaze. Eric looked amazed at her progress in marksmanship. Why this was even better than he could do himself! He was visibly moved with remorse for reprimanding her for failing to hit the trees when she first got the gun, but Sarah seemed to enjoy the situation tremendously; he had made her feel bad and now it was his turn to squirm.

Well, he was glad she could handle a gun that well, and from now on he would be less worried to leave her alone. As they were nearing the cabin Sarah burst out laughing and said; "Why you big dumb Swede! I didn't hit the bull's eyes at all, I just managed to hit the trees and then cut the blaze over the bullet holes."

"You little devil," he replied, "Why did you do this to me?"

Well, I thought this was a good way to teach you that we must trust and encourage one another if we are to survive in the wilderness, and of course I wanted to get even with you."

They both had learned their lesson, and the first shadow to fall over their wedded life dissipated before Sarah's cheerful disposition. Sarah continued with her rifle practice until she was proficient enough to shoot the head off a grouse.

Time went quickly for the busy people on the Nicomekl and after the sowing season was over Eric and Sarah resumed the afternoon walks they were accustomed to enjoying while living in Chilliwack. Both nourished a silent longing to see the ocean again, so early one morning late in July they started out for the shores of the Pacific. They followed the Native trail along the Nicomekl River and came to a delta where there were three homesteads on the south side. The couple stopped long enough to get acquainted with the new settlers, then continued on a trail that took them to Semiahmoo Bay. The trail ended at a high bluff with an unobstructed view of the bay and the far away islands. The bluff also provided a glimpse of the ocean in the far distance.

As they walked along the edge of the bluff, Eric and Sarah came to a peculiar clearing that appeared to be of man's making. It was a level plateau of about one acre, encircled by earth bulwarks or ramparts six feet high. At the front was a sheer drop to the water's edge of some one hundred feet, and on the sides, deep ravines partly filled with water. Connecting the ravines in the back was another ravine or deep ditch and it appeared as if high tide would form an island of the place.

A broad log spanned the ravine in the back, and as Sarah and Eric walked across they found the whole area littered with tent poles and clamshells. The site had the appearance of an ancient fort or bastion, but they did not know what purpose it had served. They heard that local Natives were obliging and peace loving, but did not know that warring tribes from the north were constantly attacking them. Eric and Sarah could see that this bastion had been easy to defend. An attacker would first have to swim the ravines then scale the almost perpendicular banks of loose dirt where he would be met by a barrage of rocks and arrows.

After having lunch in the shade of the six-foot ramparts, they started back to their home on the Nicomekl. Eric carried the Winchester 74 but did not have to use it. He knew that in this wild land, a gun was the only assurance of safety. The peaceful Natives, who in the past, took refuge within these ramparts could see their enemies approaching on the water. But the European settlers never knew, nor they could see their enemies lurking in the tall timber, and therefore had to be on the alert at all times.

One morning in late August while Sarah was preparing breakfast, there came a rasping at the door. When she looked out she saw a Native woman holding a baby in her arms. Sarah spoke to her, but her only answer was; "Papoose sick, Papoose sick," in a monotone, which convinced her the woman did not understand English. Sarah motioned for her to come into the cabin and took a look at the baby. From her experience with sick Native babies at Chilliwack, she recognized the symptom. The baby had been fed heavy food that his tender stomach could not digest. The fermenting food was causing terrible pain for the poor child. Sarah warmed some milk that relieved the pain. The baby went to sleep and seemed to improve as time went on. By nightfall the baby no longer cried and the mother strapped it to a pack-board, swung it onto her back and disappeared into the bush. Sarah knew that from now on she would be known as the White Medicine Woman, and would be consulted to cure any little ailment the natives might have.

About six weeks after moving from Chilliwack, the sow gave birth to seven piglets. The hens were also productive. About thirty chicks were hatched during the early summer. It was quite a problem to obtain food, so the stock had to be left to forage for itself, with the result that the hawks and eagles killed several chickens. Eric heard from other settlers that domestic geese were excellent watchdogs, so he obtained a goose and a gander from Mr. Huck at Surrey Centre.

One morning, the gander made a terrible racket, awakening both Eric and Sarah. When Eric picked up his gun and ran outside he saw a bear tearing the pigpen apart. He dropped the bear with one well-aimed shot and instead of the bear devouring the pigs, the pigs ate the bear. While Eric was away one day, Sarah spotted an eagle hovering over the clearing. She shot it on the wing, a really remarkable feat for a person who only a few months before "couldn't hit a barn door."

During the lull between the sowing and harvest seasons, Eric visited other settlers to learn the practical things that would make life and survival easier for Sarah and him in the long winter months ahead. He discovered how, by digging into a side hill, forming a chamber and lining the walls with cedar boards, he could have what they called a "root house," a place in which food could be kept fresh for a long time. He was also advised to catch trout and to salt them down for winter food. He immediately set to work making kegs from hand split spruce. Not having access to steel bands, he held the staves together with twisted willow withes and was ready for salting when the migration of fish began. As summer drew to a close, Eric could see that there would be a good crop of everything he had planted. In this virgin black loam everything grew in size and quality, like he had never seen. He thought this must be the most fertile soil in the world.

In September, word spread among the settlers that Reverend Dunn would be conducting a Christian service in the new settlement at the mouth of the river on the last Sunday of the month. Both Eric and Sarah longed to meet again the Minister who joined them in Holy Matrimony, so in the company of Mr. and Mrs. Tom Shannon, they set out for Elgin. Walking along the Mud Bay Flats, Eric pointed out the sod-roofed log cabin where he had spent two nights as a fugitive years earlier. When nearing the large McDougall[9] log cabin, where the service was to be held, the party could almost figure the size of the congregation by counting the number of guns leaning against the outside wall. The gun was an indispensable tool even while travelling to a Christian service.

Reverend Dunn was pleased to see Eric and Sarah again and to hear that they were getting on well. He said he often thought of them, as they were the first white couple he had joined in matrimony in the Valley of the Fraser. On the way home the party walked the Native trail along the south bank of the river where they noticed a number of crab apple trees. They decided to come back to pick some apples when they ripened. There were also acres of cranberries waiting to be picked. Eric found several honey bee trees from which he collected honey from time to time. It began to appear this land had everything just for the taking. Continuing along the river, the couples passed two Native camps, and when they came to the one nearest their homestead, Eric recognized several of the Natives from the previous summer. They were apparently pleased to see him again.

While Eric and Tom Shannon were talking to the men, Sarah and Mrs. Shannon became interested in the activities of the women. They were drying berries on a cedar bark mat suspended about four feet above a slow fire. The Native women related that it took three or four days to dry each batch of berries. Sarah also noticed two piles of roots which resembled potatoes and when she inquired about them, she was told that one was "camas" and the other "skous" and that they were boiled or baked in hot ashes before eaten.

Later in the fall, the people in the valley were summoned to another Christian service, this time for the funeral of a Mud Bay woman. The deceased woman was buried near the family farmhouse and the lay preacher, William Woodward, read the rituals. The homestead was abandoned shortly afterward and the place was subsequently said to be haunted.

9   John Alexander McDougall pre-empted land on the shore of the Nicomekl River in April 1877, at Elgin. His son, William, was elected to the position of Warden for Surrey in 1881, and in 1885 was elected as Surrey's Reeve.

A Trip to Semiahmoo Settlement

CHAPTER IX

For some time now Sarah had wanted to get to a store to purchase some clothing and various items needed for housekeeping. Eric and Sarah accordingly arranged to have a Native couple look after their homestead while they made a trip to the Semiahmoo settlement, on the international border.

The couple travelled along the old trail built in 1858[10] between Fort Langley and the international border. Eventually they came to a small river, which they followed to the Semiahmoo settlement. A small town nestled close to the border on the American side, but this did not make it specifically American, as most of their customers were Canadian settlers and Natives, and no customs duty[11] was imposed on any goods. To Eric and Sarah the little town looked imposing enough, although they were told it was only a shadow of its former glory.

Blaine, as the settlement was known, had been established in 1856 by the American Boundary Commission, and was incorporated on May 20, 1890. In 1858, it attained some prominence as a jumping off place for tens of thousands of miners flocking to the gold creeks of the Cariboo. Blaine also became the miners' first point of contact with civilization when they returned with their poke of gold. Here their nuggets would buy drinks to wash the alkaline dust from their parched throats, and here, too, they could buy the salacious love not generally available in the shade of the Cariboo Mountains. Or they could sit in on a friendly poker game, which sometimes ended in a free-for-all with six shooters. While many lost their fortunes and returned to the diggings for more and some met their end in gun battles, the majority made it to the civilized world and a new life.

Eric and Sarah found the stories from the past fascinating and they liked Semiahmoo so much that they decided to stay for a couple of days. Two days later, they walked out onto Semiahmoo Spit to look on the beautiful bay and the ocean, which still held an attraction for them. They had chosen to be landlubbers, but the sea around which their childhoods and youth had evolved, would always draw them like a strong magnet.

The Semiahmoo Spit was a narrow strip of land running about three quarters of a mile into the bay and was inhabited by a number of Natives headed by Chief Spas, who was said to be about one hundred and ten years old. Eric and Sarah had heard of the old sage and were curious to meet him in person. As they entered his lodge, the old man pointed to some hides on the floor and said, "sit," more as an order than an invitation. Chief Spas spoke good English and seemed to sense Eric's questions before he had a chance to ask them.

The chief began by stating how he had resented the white man's intrusion upon his domain, but now accepted it as an inevitable event in the course of history. He knew now that the world had many people who needed more room, but he was concerned about his own people assimilating into the white race. Contact with the white men had left his people less motivated to hunt and fish. Instead, young Native men would meet the sailing ships to acquire trinkets, which they in turn traded through the valley, with the result that they were left without enough food for the winter. The young women left their tribe to work in the white man's settlements, or would follow a settler to his cabin in the forest. Maybe that was good, he did not know, but he did know that his tribe had dwindled to a fraction of the size it was when he was a young man and he did not think that was good.

Eric could see the old Chief was deeply pained by concerns about his people, so in order to change the subject he told the Chief about their visit to the old fort on the North Bluff and asked him what had been its use or purpose. Eric's question appeared to please the old man, as it gave him an opportunity to delve into his most cherished subject, the legends and glories of his people's past.

"The Semiahmoo People," he said, "were kind and peace loving and the bay was teeming with fish most of the time. The woods were full of game and the bogs red with berries in the fall. Camas and skous could be dug anytime and there was always an abundance of food. Theirs would have been an ideal life if it had not been for the periodic raids from the warlike tribes of the north. "My ancestors built the fort that you saw on the high bluff, as protection for women and children, while the braves battled the marauders. They had sentries on the point yonder [Point Roberts] and on a signal from them all the women and children were taken to the fort. The last battle took place where now stands the white man's stores and hotel [Blaine]. The Haida were led by a chief with an enormously deformed head that seemed to rest on his left shoulder. The chief and many of his warriors were killed and buried on the battleground, and there has not been a raid since."

As the Chief stopped talking for a minute, Eric had thoughts that the battle must have taken place about the time Captain Vancouver first dropped anchor in Birch Bay, in 1792. "After the victory," Spas continued, "my father the chief called his council together and said he was growing old and wanted to turn the mantle over to his son. The councillors thought he had proven his ability to remain their chief, but he insisted and I was elected to take his place. I have been their Chief since then. I was not yet married so my father sent two war canoes to

Camosun [Victoria] to bring a bride for me from the Songhees tribe. When they returned my father held a Potlatch with guests from many parts of the Coast. During the celebrations, a ship came to the bay and we visited it in hundreds of canoes and received many gifts from the white sailors."

At this point the old Chief became silent, closed his eyes and appeared to be reminiscing. Eric knew the interview was over, so he and Sarah returned to the hotel. Eric said he wanted to go to their room and do some writing and suggested Sarah finish her shopping. Alone now with stories of the past parading through his poetic mind, he began putting down stanzas, which were forming from the visions. He would call this:

Ballad Of Semiahmoo Bay

Peace and quietness now descending,
Over shores of Silvery Bay,

Northern raiders were retreating,
After battle of the day.

Homeward bound, the mighty warriors,
To their village on the shore,

To sing their songs of freedom,
From this day evermore.

As the evening sun was sinking,
Into Semiahmoo Bay,
Old Chief Pallock told a story,
From a far bygone day;

"Sons," said he, "you've done your duty,
Like your fathers in the past,

Slain your foe and won the battle,
And I think peace will last.

Now go forth and bring your mothers,
From the bastion in the North,

Bring your sisters and your brothers,
From their exile at the Fort.

I shall hold a final Potlatch,
For I think my days are done,

I shall then lay down my mantle,
And your Chief shall be my Son.

Take your great canoes and journey,
On toward the midday sun,

Till you reach the Songhee Island,
Where the ocean breakers run.

Choose the loveliest of maidens,
From that old and noble tribe,

Bring her here in joy and glory,
For my Son, to be his bride.

Call my friends, the Chief of Halouk,
And Andrie of Techossem,

Call on George, the Chief of Halta,
And Chief Michael of Kwantlen.

Call as many of my Kinsmen,
Whom I hold in friendly bond,

For I soon shall start the journey,
To the Happy Hunting Ground."

When at last the Chief ceased talking,
And the braves were on their way,

There commenced a celebration,
Seldom seen on Silvery Bay.

People came from the many Nations,
Living on the West land Coast,

Came on land, on sea and rivers,
To pay homage to their host.

After having their fill of "civilization", Eric and Sarah started back to the homestead on the Nicomekl, heavily laden with store goods. On this trip they engaged two Natives with a large canoe to take them as far up the Nicomekl as it was possible to paddle. They came within a short distance of their homestead where the river was blocked by a large pile of driftwood. When arriving home they found that everything had been well taken care of by the Native couple. The man had even chopped a pile of wood. Sarah had purchased a pair of earrings and some cloth, which she presented to the woman, and Eric gave the man a hunting knife. They both appreciated the gifts and departed to their humble tent in the bush, happy as larks on a spring day.

10 In 1858 this trail was known as "Smuggler's Trail." Later the name changed to "Miner's Trail" and still later it was changed to "The Fort Langley Trail." The trail began near the mouth of the Campbell River, (Blaine) and followed the river inland for approximately ten kilometres to what is now Highway 15 and 8th Avenue in Hazelmere, in South Surrey. At this point it continued in a north-easterly direction until it crossed the Salmon River in Langley, then continued on to Fort Langley.

11 The first Customs Post was located at Port Elgin on the Nicomekl River, in the Clay (Elgin) Hotel, at the junction of the Semiahmoo Road and the Nicomekl River. In 1886, Elgin was designated as a customs entry port. The Semiahmoo Road was the main north-south transportation link from Brown's Landing to the State of Washington, U.S.A. The Nicomekl River was the main water transportation route inland to Surrey.

Flour and Coal Oil

CHAPTER X

After the harvesting was done, Eric loaded several sacks of wheat into the farm wagon and drove to the newly built mill at Brown's Landing to have it ground into flour. While waiting for the work to be done, he went across to New Westminster to buy a few things and call for the mail. Eric wanted to buy something to surprise Sarah and settled for a coal oil lamp. Until now they had used candles, but it was difficult to do any sewing in the poor light that they cast, so he knew she would appreciate a lamp. He chose a wall lamp, which had a reflector on the back, designed to spread an even light throughout the room.

BROWNSVILLE FERRY SLIP, 1902

With two five-gallon cans of coal oil acquired, Eric started back to Brown's Landing, where he picked up his flour and continued the long journey home. When nearing Clover Valley, a strong smell of coal oil made him stop and make sure the lids were tight on the containers. He had not yet built a wagon road to his homestead, so he had to stop to unload the wagon at Shannons'.

Tom Shannon came out and helped him unload, and as they lifted the first sack, it was found to be soggy with coal oil. To their horror they found that one of the cans had sprung a leak and the flour had absorbed the oil and that it was utterly useless for human consumption. It was a hard blow to Eric, as he did not have any money left to buy flour, nor was there enough grain left for another trip to the mill. It was with heavy steps that he walked over to his homestead and it would be a painful duty to telling Sarah what had happened to their flour. He knew how much she was looking forward to having all the flour she required for bread and how she planned to bake cookies and other good things. It was their intention to invite neighbours over to help celebrate Christmas in their new home.

Sarah met him at the door with a kiss, but she knew even before he spoke that there was something wrong. She listened silently while he told about the tragic misfortune. He had expected she would burst out crying and reproach him for his carelessness, but once again this woman presented true pioneer spirit. Without even mentioning their great loss, she suggested they take some of the pigs to New Westminster and trade them for some flour. Eric had not even thought of this and agreed it was a good idea. They would still have some pigs left for their own food. A few days before Christmas, Eric was once again on the corduroy road to New Westminster, where he had no difficulty disposing of the pigs for a good supply of flour.

Eric bought another can of coal oil; this time he wasn't going to take any chances, he would carry the darned thing. The five-gallon can had a narrow, sharp handle, so he had to continually shift from one hand to the other, and the cursed thing seemed to get heavier with every step. While ascending the steep hill about a mile from Brown's Landing, he was trying to figure out some way to put the can into the wagon.

FERRY "SURREY" MID-STREAM LOADED WITH BUGGIES

Eric thought of moving the flour sacks to leave a vacant spot for the can, but even that would involve some risk, which he could not afford to take. Then he came up with a bright idea; why not suspend the can under the wagon? With a piece of rope he tied the can to the cross beam of the wagon, and as he walked behind watching it hang there with hardly a motion, he became quite proud of his invention. Had he known at this time that his experiment was to become an accepted practice of many settlers, he would really have been elated. Such was the way of the pioneer; when someone learned a better method of doing things, it was readily made available to all. Without teamwork, cooperation, and mutual assistance among the pioneers, the taming of the wilderness would never have been accomplished.

Some days later, Eric and Sarah were picking berries along the edge of a prairie when they came upon the ruins of a log cabin. This had been the home of Sam Hall, who arrived in the area in 1845. Hall is believed to be the first European to settle in the district. Eric had not previously seen the cabin, although had heard the story that Sam was a trapper for Fort Langley. Hall was said to have taken a Native girl for his common-law-wife, eventually shooting her. He was convicted of murder and was executed for his crime in 1862.

"Also," Eric told Sarah, "somewhere along the edge of this prairie, another man paid the supreme penalty for murder in the year 1865. At that time, telegraph lines were being strung from the American side into New Westminster and there was a station just inside the border, which was called 'Telegraph.' One morning, the operator was found shot to death and the white men living in the vicinity formed a posse and set out after the suspected murderer. They caught up with him somewhere around here and strung him up in the nearest tree." Sarah shuddered at the weird stories and as she looked at the dilapidated log cabin, she thought it fortunate that nature in a short time would obliterate all traces of Sam Hall's presence in the area.

On the way home, Eric said he heard of settlers who had taken Native women as common-law-wives and when European women became available, "paid them off," that is, gave them a few dollars and sent them back to their families. Sarah thought this was the lowest act a man could perpetrate, particularly in view of the fact that she knew several Native women married to settlers, who had become excellent mothers and housekeepers. The Native women may not have had the same background, but they learned fast, and one Native woman Sarah knew personally was often referred to as the most respected woman in the Valley.

One evening at dusk, Eric was milking the cow. The squeal of a pig made him run outside just in time to see a bear heading toward the timber carrying a pig. Eric picked up a fence post and hit the bear with all his strength. The bear dropped the pig and attacked Eric. In an instant, the pole was knocked out of Eric's hand by the bear and a second blow from the bear sent him somersaulting towards the barn. As the bear stopped for a second, a shot rang out. The bear folded like a jack knife. With gun in hand, Sarah came running over to where Eric was trying to get up from a hunched position. Blood was streaming from his neck and shoulder, but he could still move his arm, so they did not think there were any broken bones. He was rallying quickly from his dazed condition and with Sarah's help reached the cabin where she dressed his wounds.

Sarah did not think the wound to be serious unless complications set in, but Eric would probably carry the bear's claw marks for the rest of his life. He remained silent while Sarah dressed his wounds. He was apparently suffering from shock, the shock of neglecting to carry his gun. "Thanks for saving my life," he said with a quivering voice, "I shall never again ignore the code of the wild, to carry a gun at all times."

Winter came and with it, a few inches of snow from time to time, but it never remained on the ground more than a day or two each time. On Christmas Day, some fifteen people came to visit the young couple on the Nicomekl. For most of them it was their first opportunity to meet Eric and Sarah. Mr. W. J. Brewer came from Mud Bay to inform them that several meetings had been held to discuss naming the district between the Fraser River and the International Boundary. He said he had suggested the name "Surrey" due to the geographic similarity of the district to the County of Surrey in England, as well as due to its relationship to Westminster. Those present at meetings on the subject had approved of the name. Brewer had been instructed to place the matter before the government in Victoria, and as he did not expect any opposition, he advised everyone to use Surrey, New Westminster as his or her address. Until now the postal address had been New Westminster District, which caused much delay and confusion, as there were several other districts in the vicinity without any other identity.

New Year's Day 1881 passed much like any other day on the homestead by the Nicomekl. The regular chores took the best part of the day and before retiring, Eric put the first cross on the new almanac. Only by conscientiously marking off each day could they keep track of time. One dreary day followed another throughout the winter, but even the rain and mist rolling in from the Pacific could not mar the contentment of the young pioneers. They lived in complete harmony with their environment and their busy life left no room for loneliness.

Nature provided them with abundance beyond compare. They were the rulers of the forest, constantly proceeding through their work, thus being masters of their own fate. The little clearing on the bend of the river, which the young fugitive had called "home" a few years before, had now grown into fields and meadows with the assurance of a prosperous life.

The Coming Of Spring

CHAPTER XI

With the coming of spring, Eric and Sarah resumed their Sunday afternoon walks through the district, often visiting nearby homesteads. Sarah had often expressed a desire to see the historic Hudson's Bay Company post at Fort Langley, so one Sunday the couple ventured out toward the fort.

ORIGINAL FORT
Fort Langley in 1894

During the winter, Eric had constructed a fourteen foot boat, which they rowed up river until they came to the Tsakawayan Portage over which the Natives had travelled for untold generations when going to the fishing grounds on the Fraser. The first Europeans also used this Portage in 1824, when they arrived to survey for the Hudson's Bay trading post on the Fraser River. Chief Clerk John Work described the portage as a "knee-deep quagmire in its entire length." But now, fifty years later, it was covered with a carpet of grass, which made for easy walking.

Arriving at the fort, Eric and Sarah were admitted inside the palisade and given a tour of the grounds by the Chief Factor. Mr. Thompson told them that the fort was now only a shadow of its former importance and it appeared only a matter of time before it would be closed completely.[12] Thompson then took them to the bastion and showed them the swivel guns which had helped to prevent a massacre in 1837. "At that time," he said, "a large armada of Yuculta warriors from Seymour Narrows attacked the Fort, but their canoes were literally blown out of the water by these guns."[13] Thompson also told them about the activities in the early days when salmon and cranberries were packed in barrels and shipped to many parts of the world. Another profitable export had been isinglass made from the bladders of the large sturgeon, which were abundant in the river during the early days. Mr. Thompson said the Natives had an ingenious contraption by which they caught sturgeon on the spawning grounds. It consisted of a pole or sometimes several poles fitted together. On the end was a type of harpoon made from bones or tree roots and a rope was attached to the other end.

With this device the Natives were able to catch sturgeon weighing up to eight hundred pounds. Sometimes it took them days to play the fish out and get them ashore. Mr. Thompson related how in 1858 the fort took regal splendour when James Douglas was proclaimed Governor of the new Colony of British Columbia. "Also at that time," he said, "the fort became the outfitting and jumping off post for thousands of miners flocking to the gold creeks of the Cariboo. But there were also times of hardship when the river froze over, preventing normal shipping."

HUDSON'S BAY STORE
Store at Fort Langley in 1880

Eric and Sarah were both glad they had visited the old fort, for stories from the past gave colour and encouragement to their life. They both came from countries steeped in history and legend. Their inherited curiosity drove them to learn all they could about the history of their adopted land.

Shortly after they arrived back at the homestead, Mr. Brewer called, carrying a petition to the government, lobbying for the incorporation of the district into a municipality. Brewer asked Eric if he could find time to canvas along the Fraser River for signatures. For some time, Eric had been looking for an excuse to go down to visit settlements along the Fraser River. He had reason to believe that one of his partners from his sailing days had settled there, and was longing to see him again. He had told no one, except Sarah, about the fellow sailors who had jumped ship with him in 1872, and this assignment would give him an opportunity to look them up without arousing suspicion.

A short distance below the homestead, Eric came upon some trees that bore traces of old blazes. He knew he was on the right track. This was the Coast Meridian survey line that the Royal Engineers had cut around 1860, and now, almost twenty years later, only large bubbles of pitch remained of the first land survey on the lower mainland of British Columbia. Eric followed the blazes due north and soon came upon a well-travelled trail that testified that settlers coming into the district had used it. After crossing the Yale Wagon Road, an obscure trail took him to the Fraser. A short distance from the river, he came to the homestead of the former partner and the pleasure of meeting after many

THE VALLEY OF THE FRASER

years separation was mutual. Albert Anderson had settled in the district known as Port Kells, had cleared a large tract of land, and had done well due to easy access to river transportation and the market in New Westminster. The third fugitive from the old schooner had headed for the United States and was never heard of again.

Eric remained overnight with his old partner and the next day located a few scattered settlers along the river, who were glad to sign the petition. When he came to Brown's Landing he discovered that several who had pre-empted land there lived in New Westminster which meant he had to cross the river to get their signatures on the petition. As he returned home, Eric felt that his mission had been successful. He had seventeen signatures on the petition, and thought that the twenty-four required additional signatures could be attained from the settlers of the Nicomekl Valley.

12 Construction of the first Fort Langley began on August 1st 1827, as a Hudson's Bay Company post. In 1858, Fort Langley achieved prominence as the starting point for travel to the Fraser River gold fields. In August 1858, the British Parliament revoked the Hudson's Bay Company monopoly and passed an act creating the British Columbian mainland a British Crown Colony. James Douglas was proclaimed the first Governor for the Colony of British Columbia. The inaugural ceremony, although honouring Fort Langley, also signalled the fort's decline. The palisade was dismantled in 1864, and in 1872 the "Big House" was demolished. In April 1886, after 59 years of loyal service, the fort ceased operations.

13 One early evening in 1837, the Fort Langley guns roared in anger. More than one thousand Yuculta Natives paddled up the Fraser River to attack the Kwantlen located alongside the Fort. Chief Whattlekainum's peaceful Kwantlen village was under attack by the Yucultan. It was just before dusk and the Fort's sentries yelled, the cannons were loaded, swivel guns armed, and muskets prepared for use. The Kwantlen villagers fled to the forests and when the war canoes came into range of the Fort's armaments, a signal was given to 'fire.' Canoes were blasted apart by the shelling, warriors flailed in the river, swimming frantically into the main river channel. Many were drowned. The Kwantlen emerged from the forest and with clubs and knives to massacre many Yuculta. Never thereafter did the Yuculta threaten life in the Valley of the Fraser.

Incorporation of Surrey Municipality

CHAPTER XII

W. J. Brewer presented the petition for incorporation to the Government in Victoria, and on 10 November 1879, the district was incorporated as the Municipal District of Surrey. The Letters Patent incorporated an area of 132 square miles, with less than forty white people living within its boundaries.

During the late 1870s, a large logging camp started operating on Hall's Prairie and Eric worked there as a carpenter from time to time. The camp paid good wages and, in addition, purchased all the farm produce the homesteaders could spare. Eric lived at home while working at the mill, and in the evenings would tell Sarah about the happenings in the camp. He said that the company had hundreds of Chinese men digging a ditch, or canal, from the Nicomekl River for two and one half miles into the woods. When the canal was finished, logs would be floated down to the Nicomekl.

From the top of the canal the company were constructing skid roads in several directions into the big timber. A ten-foot roadbed was graded through the woods. Logs were then laid crossways over it, spaced nine feet apart and partly bedded into the ground. Over these skids the big logs were hauled by teams of oxen and were to be dumped into the canal.

For the past year, Eric had been working, when opportunity permitted, on building a substantial farmhouse. After the sowing season in 1880, he finished the roof on the house and installed the windows, which he obtained in New Westminster, through the logging company. One evening when they were discussing moving into the new house, Sarah said that he had it ready just in time, as they would soon have company. At first he did not appear to grasp what she was hinting at, but as the light finally dawned on him, he did not seem too happy about the prospect. It had been just the two of them for so long that they had moulded into a happy, harmonious entity and he was concerned about anything breaking it up. In his subconscious mind he had always envisioned life continuing as the glorious dream it had been.

Eric sat deep in thought, and intuition told Sarah he was fighting an emotion new and strange to him. He had difficulty reconciling the fact that he was about to become a father, but after all, it could not be considered an accident after all these years of wedded harmony. When he finally embraced and kissed her, it reminded Sarah of his first, tender kiss that August evening on top of Lovers' Leap.

The days that followed made a big change in Eric's attitude toward Sarah. No longer would he let her carry water from the creek, nor would he pass up an opportunity to wait on her. This did not particularly please Sarah, as she felt quite capable of carrying on her regular work, and when Eric suggested making arrangements for her admittance to the hospital at Sapperton, she became very angry. She would not be any different from other pioneer women who had their babies at home. She had confidence in Mrs. Shannon as a midwife and would have no part of going to the hospital.

After moving into the new house, Eric and Sarah often looked toward the little log cabin with nostalgic memories. Within its cramped quarters they had been so close to each other, but here in the large, empty rooms of the new house, they both had a feeling of drifting apart. To Eric, the little log cabin had a great deal of meaning. It was the first tangible result of his labour and skill in this west land, and within its rough timber walls he had experienced the happiest years of his life.

ANDERSON CABIN, 2005
At Surrey Museum.

As twilight descended once again over their new home on the Nicomekl, Eric felt an urge in his soul to do something in appreciation for everything the little cabin gave him. He would try to write a poem in its memory, a poem that would live forever.

My Cabin In The Pines

Shielded in the heart of the forest,
Framed by the river and stream,
Hewed from the giants of ages,
Which grew when the west was a dream,

Here on the knoll by the river,
The picturesque log cabin stands,
It gave me shelter and haven,
In a strange and mysterious land.
Scarred from the ravage of winter,

Bleached by the midsummer sun,
Drenched by the rain from the ocean,

At last, its days are now done.

But I shall forever remember,
The happiness, solace and rest,
As a gift from the little log cabin,
My first real home in the West.

As the years rolled by, the little clearing on the Nicomekl continued expanding, until it eventually became one of the biggest farms in the district. Steamboats plied the Nicomekl River, loading produce for the markets in Victoria and New Westminster and towing log booms to the mills. Civic government came to the district, and the first Municipal Council meeting was held in the Shannon home at Clover Valley on January 12, 1880. The 132 square mile municipality was divided into seven wards, represented by seven Councillors, with Tom Shannon serving as the first Warden.

Although Eric never consented to stand for election to Council, he attended its meetings and noted many humorous transactions over the years. At the very first meeting he noted that Ebenezer Brown, Councillor for Brown's Landing[14], served notice of intent to apply for a liquor licence for his hotel at the next meeting. The inference seemed to be that he had been bootlegging up until that time, but now that he had become a duly elected councillor, he had to appear to be more respectable. At another meeting complaints were received from irate citizens of Brown's Landing, noting that a hotel keeper (not Brown), was making homebrew in his backyard and selling it to local people, while he favoured strangers with good whiskey.

By 1883, the little Native village that Eric first visited in 1872 had become the biggest settlement south of the Fraser River. It had a large fish cannery, some stores, three hotels and two "sporting houses." There were constant problems between the two sporting houses, and from time to time reports would reach the Council about people mysteriously disappearing, but nothing was ever proven that could be acted upon.

The government eventually appointed a sheriff, in the person of a moonshine-producing hotelkeeper, whose wife was the proprietor of one of the sporting houses. This combination did not lend itself to any improvement in law enforcement. The lone police officer appointed by Municipal Council was often hampered by the practice of New Westminster lawmen to give undesirables the "floater," that is, to exile them to the wilderness of Surrey. Often a dangerous criminal would escape across the river and hide out in the tall timber, where the lone constable would have to flush him out. It is said that this officer never carried a gun while on duty, but always got his man. How he did it, no one knew.

At one time the municipal policeman was requested by the New Westminster police to bring in an escaped murderer. He met the criminal in the big timber above Surrey Centre and talked him into surrendering. After a lodging him in the "lock-up," the outlaw said, "Mr. Police, if you had come for me with a gun, you would have been a dead man now."

In July 1883, Eric and Sarah were summoned to the funeral of Mrs. Pike, at Mud Bay. People came from many parts of Surrey and the occasion took on the nature of a mid-summer festival; "everyone had a good time at poor Mrs. Pike's funeral." All guests stayed overnight, the men and the boys sleeping in the hayloft and the women on the floor of the Lamb family's large farmhouse nearby. After the festivities, the body was carried manually over the Semiahmoo Trail for interment at Semiahmoo. When Eric took his turn as pallbearer, he kept thinking about the history of this trail. His Native friends had told him that their ancestors journeying from the winter camps on the coast to the fishing grounds on the Fraser used it for untold generations. Now, the trail was no longer resounding to the beat of the Native's moccasins and in a few more years nature would completely obliterate all trace of it. When the procession crossed the Nicomekl River and started up the side hill, it passed a large freshwater well where the Natives had camped while gathering shellfish. This well was also a significant source of drinking water for the settlers living on the Mud Bay flats.

Eric became deeply engrossed in the legends and history of the old trail, and when he arrived home he attempted to express his feelings in a poem:

The Old Semiahmoo Trail

Ere a Paleface saw this West land,
In its beauty by the sea,
Indian mothers crooned their love songs,
To a race both brave and free.
Bronzed and beautiful they wandered,
Heedless of the wild land's gale -
Sang their soft and tender ditties,
On the Semiahmoo Trail.

Theirs the only voice of human,

In the vastness of the West;
Theirs the only footprints leading
From shores to mountain crest,
Free and happy at their campfires,

Free and brave on war's wild trail -
How they sang their songs of freedom,
On the Semiahmoo Trail.

Then one day a white sail glimmered,
On the silvery waters crest -
T'was the coming of the Paleface,

To this garden in the West.
Now the trail is lone and dreary,
Only ghosts of yore bewail,
The passing of the Redman,
From the Semiahmoo Trail.

Anon.

14 Brown's Landing is located in the South Westminster area of Surrey. Eric and his partners came ashore at what is today Tannery Road. For many years there was a tannery at the site and a dock was established for the Norwegian fishermen in South Westminster to moor their fishing boats and to repair their fish nets. There were several canneries along the Fraser River foreshore, beginning at the Surrey/Delta border and continuing to Brownsville. The early fishermen and their families lived in homes along the river foreshore, in this location.

Semiahmoo
Trail Cairn
1961

Schools in
The Forest

CHAPTER XIII

As settlers continued to arrive in the district, they were faced by a new problem; that of teaching their children the Three "R's." Many new arrivals came from Eastern Canada, where their children had attended public school, but here in the West they were left to roam like denizens of the forest. Some of the earliest settlers became heedful of the situation and called a meeting on the subject of school during the summer of 1882. The meeting was held on a cedar windfall log along McLellan Road and a delegation was appointed to place the matter before the government in Victoria. The government subsequently agreed to supply a teacher if the settlers provided the schoolhouse and its furniture.

The first school in Surrey was a one-room shack, donated by a bachelor named Robinson. The building was located near the southwest corner of what is now 176th Street and 60th Avenue. There is a rock cairn with a bronze plaque on the northeast corner of the intersection commemorating the first school site.

By September 1882, the government sent a teacher, in the person of Mary Jane Norris, from Langley, to begin the duty of educating future generations of Surreyites. The first class consisted of twelve pupils, all members of the Boothroyd, Huck, Shannon, and Thrift families. A year later, the shack became too small, and the schoolhouse was relocated to an acre of land donated and fenced by Joe Shannon. The pupils' fathers made its desks and chairs. The site later became home to the Zion Lutheran Church and school on 60th Avenue.

From 1883 to 1900, the provincial government erected schools in every part of Surrey; most of them being one-room log structures. School District No. 36, which covered Surrey, White Rock, and the unorganized area of Barnston Island, was incorporated in 1906.

Then Came The Churches

CHAPTER XIV

Whether the pioneers were more pious than their descendants is questionable, but the fact remains that the church was often the first and only place early settlers could meet and associate with their fellow men. After the building of the first Municipal Hall at Surrey Centre in 1881, a site was chosen for the first church in the municipality. The man charged with building the church was Rev. William Bell, a graduate of Trinity College, Toronto. Bell had come to British Columbia in 1881, building St. Alban's church at Ladner shortly after his arrival. Bell was a bachelor and lived in a log cabin on the Fraser riverbank, but some of the Native mothers could not see the virtue of a man living alone and were forever offering to redress the situation. One mother even went so far as to sit on a windfall in front of his cabin for two days and essentially held him prisoner in his own home.

In 1883, Reverend Bell was transferred to Surrey Centre and instructed to build an Anglican church, but no provision was made for the funds he required to purchase the required land, lumber, shingles, and hardware. Abraham Huck subsequently donated seven acres of land on a hillside covered by beautiful evergreens. Lumber was obtained from the Royal City Sawmills, then towed downriver from New Westminster, around Point Roberts, from the Fraser River, then up the Serpentine River to the foot of the hill. A team of oxen then hauled it to the building site. Several mills operating in the area donated shingles for the roof and the settlers themselves performed most of the construction labour. The Anglican Diocese of New Westminster paid for the church's doors, windows, and hardware. The church's cornerstone was placed on Wednesday, August 16th 1884, and the first service was held seven weeks later.

Some of the land was consecrated as a burial ground and when deaths and tragedy occurred, the settlers no longer had to carry the deceased over forest trails to some far away cemetery.

CHRIST CHURCH,
SEPTEMBER, 1884

He Found
His Missing Rib

CHAPTER XV

While the church was under construction, Rev. Bell had remained a bachelor, stubbornly resisting the overtures of European mothers with eligible daughters. One day in July 1884, when Eric was working in the bottom field at his homestead, Rev. Bell came walking by and stopped to pass the time of day. Eric was somewhat surprised to see the vicar in this part of the valley and could not resist asking the question, "And where is the Reverend heading for now?" Bell was quick to reply, "Oh! I am going across the border to pick up my missing rib!" (See Genesis 2:22).

A few days later, Bell returned in the company of Georgina Carey. Miss Carey was originally from Meadford, Ontario, and was Bell's boyhood sweetheart. The newly married couple settled down in Surrey Centre where they raised eight children, each of who became a prominent British Columbian citizen.

Reverend
Alexander Bell

Stark Tragedy In the Forest

CHAPTER XVI

Tragedy and death struck often in the virgin forest of Surrey, but such events were seldom recorded and therefore failed to go down in history.

Eric was told the story of four miners who started out on a blind trail from Semiahmoo to Fort Langley in 1858, but got lost at Clayton Hill, a short distance above his homestead. While wandering about trying to find their way out, they came upon a body. On the man's chest was pinned a small note bearing the inscription:

> *July 6, 1858, three days without food or water. J. R. Dillerton of Sacramento City.*

The men who found the body were themselves too exhausted to attend to its burial. When they finally reached Fort Langley, they were almost naked and in such poor physical condition, that it took several days for them to recuperate.

Time and again Eric heard about settlers being killed by large trees they were burning down, reminding him of the close call he had when a tree demolished his cabin. In 1885 he was personally involved again when a neighbour, Mr. J. W. Figg, became a victim. Mr. Figg, like many other settlers, would call for his mail at Hall's Prairie every Sunday. One day, when Figg failed to show up, Eric went to his homestead to investigate. He found his neighbour's body well clear of a fallen tree but eventually concluded that Figg had been killed by a flying snag.

On March 29th 1887, a tragedy struck which put a shadow of gloom over the entire district. Many knew a young boy from Surrey Centre, Teddy Wade, who often played on a raft in the Serpentine River. On that dreadful day, while jumping ashore, Teddy got caught in a mud bank. The harder he tried to free himself, the deeper he sank. Someone who took them as a boy's prank heard his frantic cries for help, and Teddy Wade was left to his terrible fate. The friendly tide, which so often had carried him up and down the river, now turned its ugly face and mercilessly covered him inch by inch, until only a ripple of his last breath remained.

It was customary in those days for some local scribe to compose a song or poem about sorrowful tragedies and Eric had already started a poem in memory of Teddy Wade, when his attention was drawn to one written by J. W. Walker, a former Reeve of Surrey. Eric thought Mr. Walker had told the dramatic story well, and he copied it down:

In Memory Of Teddy Wade

Deep lie the waters in the vale.
The Serpentine is out;
And not a yard, but you might sail
And tack and turn about.

The Cypress swamp dark and still,
Save blue-jay's screech so harsh;
A lonely crane, all legs and bill,
Stands dreaming in the marsh.

Above the floods the willow bend,
As though by sorrow swayed,

*Reminded of the mournful end
Of little Teddy Wade.*

*His parents' eldest son was he,
A bright and clever boy,
Just getting old enough to be
His father's pride and joy.*

*One day he sent him to Holenroyed,
To honour Buck and Bright,
And never feared, nor felt annoyed,
To see him not at night.*

*To stay till morn he might be pressed,
As he would often do,
A well-known and well loved guest;
The ocean knew him too.*

*The morning came, never more
Came Teddy home again,
Until there entered by the door
A melancholy train.*

*They found him 'neath the swollen tide,
Laid in the river bed,
They left him by his own bedside,
All that was mortal dead.*

*In Christ Church yard, in mother earth,
He sleeps upon the breast,
Of Mother Church, by Second Birth,
With all the Saints at rest.*

*And when the floods come o'er the land,
And winter 'gins to fade,
While standing sadly on the strand
We think of Teddy Wade.*

– Festom S. Georgii, 1887 – W. J. W.

Teddy Wade Headstone, 1887

Down to the
Sea Again

CHAPTER XVII

Aside from an occasional trip to New Westminster, Eric and Sarah had not been away from their homestead overnight for ten years. In the summer of 1890, they decided on a holiday at the popular Blackie Spit. This time they could not pack up and go as they had in the past. They had three youngsters to consider. The problem was solved in a typical pioneer way. They loaded the farm wagon with a week's provisions, placed the children on top of the bed clothes, tied a milk cow behind the wagon, and set out for the playground by the ocean. They arrived there in time for the Dominion Day celebration and found several families camped along the Spit.

ANDERSON FAMILY
C. 1890

One evening, an old-timer told Eric a story he thought worth noting. He said that in 1873, the famous judge H. P. Pellew Crease had purchased 160 acres near the Spit, from someone who had previously pre-empted it, and had constructed a hunting lodge, which was maintained by a Native valet.

Judge Crease was a great sportsman and an outstanding oarsman, who spent much of his spare time at the Spit. He constructed a duck blind on an islet between the mouth of the Nicomekl and the Spit. One morning, while waiting for the duck flight to begin, his valet spotted a Native canoe setting out from the opposite shore on what appeared to be a not too friendly visit.

The storyteller claimed that Judge Crease had recently convicted a Semiahmoo Native for murder and the approaching party was out to avenge the hanging of their friend. As the war party was cutting off their retreat to shore, Judge Crease decided to rely on his oarsmanship and set out across the Bay. Even though he was rowing with super-human effort, the sleek Native canoe was gaining in the race. The situation looked grim for the honourable gentleman. But where brawn failed, brains persisted. When the pursuing canoe came within point blank range, the Judge picked up his heavy gauge shotgun and blasted the paddles out of the Natives' hands. He reached the safety of Point Roberts and there is no record of any further troubles.

The old timer also told Eric that when he first came to Blackie Spit, there were cedar boxes hanging in the trees. Inside the boxes were human remains. But now the boxes were removed and the remains had been re-buried in a common grave.

After the glorious holiday at Blackie Spit, the family started back to their homestead on the Nicomekl. On the way they called at Elgin, where, so many years ago, Eric and Sarah had attended the first Christian service in the district. Now the place had two hotels and a store, with a stagecoach passing through twice a week while travelling between New Westminster and Bellingham.

Civilization was gradually pushing back the frontiers. The old log cabin where Eric had found shelter as a fugitive had now been replaced by rambling farm buildings. Where Native people had sat chanting around their campfires ages ago, grain now swayed in the breeze.

The old order was changing, "What will the new hold?" Eric was wondering. In 1891, new development brought a railroad through the district, greatly facilitating the shipping of fresh farm produce to the markets. Sawmills sprang up along the tracks, providing extra income for those settlers who were able to work inside them. Thrashing machines appeared; doing away with the drudgery of thrashing grain with manually operated wooden flails.

Steam engines replaced oxen and horses on the skid roads and started the universal high-lead system. This in turn created the "high-rigger," a man of daring and skill who would top a tree 100 feet from the ground and install pulleys and steel cable by which logs were hauled to a loading platform.

The railway, known as the New Westminster Southern, opened a heavily forested area called Tynehead. One evening when Eric was attending a Council meeting, a request was received from a lumber company in New Westminster for a subsidy of $2,500 to move its steam mill to Tynehead. Although the proposal would have given much needed work to the new settlers, Council did not have the money, and the request was declined. However, saw and shingle mills eventually located among the big timbers and the district became one of the most prosperous of the pioneer settlements.

Whenever Councillors had a few dollars, the cash was kept in a cigar box on the Council table and picked up by the last person leaving. At one meeting Eric noted that a poor farmer requested compensation for his horse, which he claimed had fallen through a rotten bridge, breaking its leg. There was not enough money in the cigar box, so the Councillors dipped into their own pockets and made up the balance.

Road building came into full stride with Provincial Legislative Assembly, during the sessions of 1873 and 1874, allocating funds for the construction of arterial roadways south of the Fraser River. These roads were constructed under tender, and included

Scott Road, McLellan Road, Semiahmoo Road, and Yale Road. The settlers themselves graded sixteen-foot wide gravel roads adjacent to their properties with little or no assistance from the senior government. In 1880, a settler doing roadwork in Surrey with his own equipment was paid $1.50 for a ten-hour day of roadwork. Two days spent road building with a team, or four days without a team, paid a settler's taxes for one year. There was no municipal tax on improvements for many years.

In the late 1800s, education was still limited to grade eight in the one room log schools, but some of the wealthier families sent their children to boarding schools in New Westminster and Victoria, where many completed grade twelve. All of Eric and Sarah's children graduated from high school in New Westminster.

ANDERSON BUGGY

During 1894, Major and Mrs. Robert M. Hornby arrived from England and started an Agricultural Institute south of Nicomekl River. The Hornbys became quite the business proprietors in the district by developing a method of dehydrating onions, carrots, and potatoes for the Klondike market during the gold rush of 1898.

THE HORNBY HOME

While in Surrey, Mr. Hornby became concerned about the number of young remittance men aimlessly drifting around the country and decided to do something about the situation. The result was a school where they were taught to be gentlemen farmers. A remittance man was usually the son of a well-to-do Old Country family, who failed to conform to strict Victorian customs, and was consequently sent to the Colonies to prevent further embarrassment to his family. Most such young men had good educations, but were utterly lacking of any practical training, and often became itinerant workers in the district.

Eric would often tell the story about the remittance man who got the job of swabbing the skid road with fish oil at the Gilley Brothers logging camp in Elgin. On the second day he approached Walter Gilley and asked for his time. "Why, what's the matter, don't you like the job?" asked Mr. Gilley. "Oh the job is alright, but I don't like the name associated with it." To the average citizen, the swabber was known as a 'Grease Monkey,' but the loggers had an unprintable name for the position.

When she first arrived from England, Mrs. Hornby carried a cherished floor lamp with a bright red shade. It was a beauty to behold when lit up at night behind the large living room window, like a beacon guiding travellers over the forest trails. Time and time again young fellows would knock on the front door and ask to see the "girls." When Mrs. Hornby said she had no girls, they hastily retreated into the night. These nocturnal visitations puzzled Mrs. Hornby, until she mentioned it to Sarah, who told her that the beautiful floor lamp was the cause of the whole thing. Sarah told her that in this land a red light was the hallmark of a "sporting house," and as long as she displayed the lamp near the window, she would probably continue to be visited by lovelorn loggers.

The Last Picnic

CHAPTER XVIII

Year after year, the Andersons continued to attend the community picnics at Blackie Spit, and to meet old friends and get acquainted with new settlers. Perhaps Eric and Sarah were still drawn to the ocean, which had played such a great part of their lives during earlier years. Although their children were grown, the oldest son William was twenty years of age, Eric Edwin was eighteen, and daughter Sarah Ann was sixteen, they still enjoyed the summer celebration.

On July 1st 1902, the children were gathered on the beach, watching a boat approach from East Delta, which they hoped was carrying "Honest John" Oliver and his customary pail of candy, while the elders assembled around the campfire and the official brewer of tea, John Stewart of Elgin, worked

ANDERSON CHILDREN
C. 1903

at his artistry. John Oliver had moved from his alder bottom in Surrey and had taken up land in Delta, which in a short time made him a prosperous man. In addition, he had entered provincial politics and the pail of candy may have been a mild bribe for votes among the children's parents.

This family picnic was the last the family from the Nicomekl attended together. On September 16th 1902, Sarah was not feeling well. Eric helped her into the buggy and drove the four miles to Doctor A. L. Kendall's office in Cloverdale. He then assisted her as she stepped down from the buggy and watched her as she walked up to Dr. Kendall's door. Sarah went to knock on the door; but suddenly collapsed, falling dead on the grass in front of the door. It was a terrible shock and Eric had to travel back home alone, to tell the children that their mother was gone. The doctor's diagnosis was an embolism or blood clot to the heart. Sarah's funeral was held two days later.

ERIC ANDERSON
C. 1911

The passing of his life's mate left Eric in a daze and for a long time he walked the forest trails where he had strolled hand in hand with his loved one. Often he ended up at the last resting place of his beloved wife. The children remained on the farm for some time and helped their father attain a measure of prosperity. As time went by Eric gradually overcame his sorrow and was able to resume his role in society. He re-married late in life and started a new family. By this time, the children of his first marriage were well established and had started families of their own. He found pleasure in this extended family life and thrived in the company of his children and grandchildren.

On July 15th 1911, it was thirty-nine years, almost to the day, since the young sailor from the battered old schooner stumbled onto the meadow along the Nicomekl River. While he was haying in the bottom field, surrounded by his children and grandchildren, Eric staggered and slumped down onto a pile of newly mown hay and drifted into eternal sleep.

ERIC'S FUNERAL SERVICE
Held at the Anderson Family residence, July 17th, 1911

Epilogue

Eric re-married on March 4th 1904, to Sigvoon (Runney) Siggurdsen. His second wife, a sparkling-eyed woman, was a fellow Scandinavian, having been born in Iceland. They had two children, Ellen and Henry Anderson.

In 1909, the British Columbia Electric Railway Company approached Eric and his neighbour, Alexander Anderson, to ask for some of their land for the railway they were building. Eric agreed to provide land to the company provided there would be a station, named for his family, located on the land. The railway agreed and the station, dubbed Anderson, was subsequently built. The railway also paid him $996.15 in return for the land he had sold it.

Eric, Runney, Ellen and Henry Anderson c. 1906

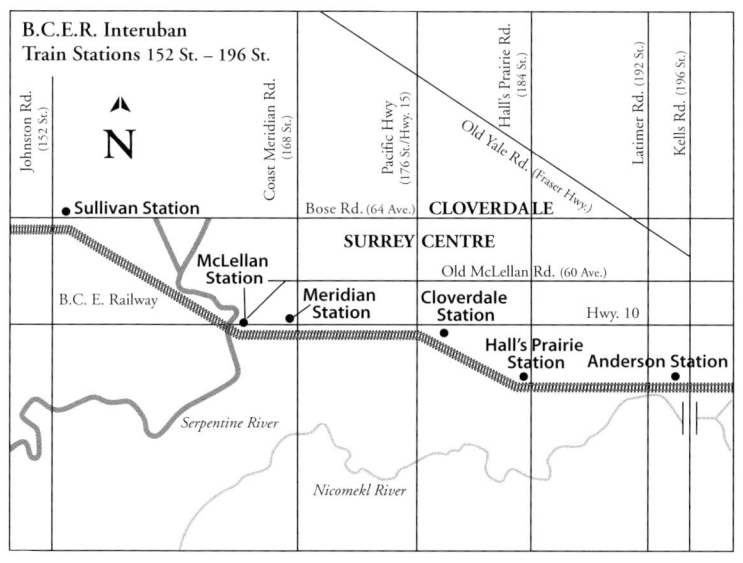

Map of BCER Stations

THE VALLEY OF THE FRASER

B.C. Electric Tram
B.C. Electric tram near Anderson Station.

In 1967, Mr. And Mrs. William Sweet purchased the Anderson homestead and the old cabin was rediscovered. In 1970, the Sweets donated the cabin to the Surrey Museum. Eric's cabin is the oldest cabin remaining in Surrey, and has now been preserved at the Museum in Cloverdale, as an historic monument to the memory of all Surrey Pioneers. An inscription at the cabin reads:

> *This simple log structure reminds us of the hard work*
> *of early settlers and the contributions made by the*
> *men and women who laid the foundations of the City*
> *we live in today.*

Photo Credits

Cover – Anderson Family,
City of Surrey Archives, 170A05

iv – Eric Anderson, c. 1872,
City of Surrey Archives, 170A01

iv – Sarah McClinton,
Cathy Brohman

p.2 – Schooner, Burrard Inlet, c. 1872
B.C. Archives and Records Service, A-00179

p.2 – Map – surrey's historic rivers and trails
Based on a sketch by Lorne Pearson

p.7 – Surrey-Langley Road, c. 1875
Cathy Brohman

p.10 – Pioneer Cabin
Lorne Pearson

p.15 – Wells Farm, c. 1895
Chilliwack Archives, P3542

p.24 – Reverend and Mrs. Dunn
Don Waite Collection

p.33 – Waterfront Scene, Halland Sweden

p.37 – Murrays' Corners, c. 1890
Langley Centennial Museum, #2668

p.38 – Home in the West
Sketch by Laurie Pearson

p.42 – Crown Title (excerpt)

p.55 – Brownsville Ferry Slip, 1902
City of Surrey Archives, 180.6.01

p.57 – Ferry "Surrey", mid-stream loaded with buggies
City of Surrey Archives, 209.08

p.61 – Original Fort, Fort Langley, 1894
Langley Centennial Museum, #1087

p.63 – Hudson's Bay Store at Fort Langley, 1880
Langley Centennial Museum, #1087

p.67 – Anderson Cabin, 2005
Lorne Pearson

p.72 – Semiahamoo Trail Cairn, 1961
Lorne Pearson

p.76 – Christ Church, September 1884
City of Surrey Archives, 50.01

p.78 – Reverend Alexander Bell
City of Surrey Archives, 170.B.15

p.82 – Teddy Wade Headstone, 1887
Surrey Museum

p.83 – Anderson Family, c. 1890
City of Surrey Archives, 170.A.05

p.86 – Anderson Buggy
Cathy Brohman

p.87 – Hornby Home
City of Surrey Archives, 170.H.19

p.88 – Anderson Children, c. 1903
Cathy Brohman

p.89 – Eric Anderson, c. 1911
Cathy Brohman

p.90 – Eric's Funeral Service, July 17, 1911
Cathy Brohman

p.91 – Eric, Runney, Ellen and Henry Anderson
Cathy Brohman

p.91 – Map of BCER Stations
Based on a sketch by
Lorne Pearson

p.92 – B.C. Electric Tram
Langley Centennial Museum, #35

INDEX

A

American Boundary
  Commission, 3, 40, 49
Anderson, Albert, 5, 64
Anderson, Alexander, Epilogue
Anderson Station, Epilogue
Andrie of Techossem, 53
Anglican Diocese of New
  Westminster, 76

B

Barnston Island, 74
B. C. Electric Railway
  Company, Epilogue
Bell, Rev. William, 74-78
Bentwick, Introduction
Bergh, Captain, 2
Birch Bay, 51
Blackie Spit, 83, 89
Blaine, 49, 51, 54
Booth, John, Introduction
Boothroyd, 74
Brewer, W. J., 59, 63
Brigade Trail, 14, 16, 27, 30
Britain, Introduction
British Columbia, 16, 19,
  35, 38, 62-63, 75, 77
British North America, 1, 35
Brohman, Katherine (Cathy),
  Acknowledgements
Brown, Ebenezer, 68
Brown's Landing, 42, 54 -
  57, 64, 68, 71
Burial ground, 11-12
Burrard Inlet, Introduction, 2, 3

C

California, 16
Campbell River, 3, 54
Camosum, 52
Camus, 48, 47
Canada, 73
Canadian, 40, 49
Carey, Georgina, 77
Cariboo, 11,14, 19-22, 36, 49-50,62
Cedar boxes, 11
Charcoal, 13
Chilliwack, Introduction, 13-14,
  16, 29-32, 34-35, 37, 39, 44, 46
Chinese, 65
Christ Church, 76, 81
City of Surrey, Introduction
City of Surrey Council,
  Acknowledgement
Clayton, 79
Cloverdale, Introduction,
  37, 90, Epilogue
Clover Valley, 37, 56, 68
Coast Meridian, 63, Epilogue
Coqualeetza, 16, 63
Crease, Judge H. P. Pellew, 83-84
Customs Post, 54

D

Dillerton, J. R., 79
Dominion Day, 83
Douglas, Governor James,
  Forward, 62, 64
Dunn, Reverend Alexander,
  23-24, 29, 47

E
East Delta, 89
Edenbank, Introduction, 16
Elgin, 47, 54, 84, 87, 89
Elliott, Alva, Acknowledgements
England, Forward, Introduction, 34, 87-88
Enniskillen County, Introduction
Europeans, 1, 5, 7-8, 14, 22-23, 25, 42, 45, 57-58, 77

F
Father of British Columbia, Forward
Figg, J. W., 79-80
Fire pit, 5
Fort Langley, 14, 16, 49, 54, 58, 61, 64, 79
Fort Yale, 14
Fraser Canyon, 27-28, 36
Fraser delta, 38
Fraser River, 12, 20, 23, 31, 42, 59, 62-64, 68-69, 71, 75, 78, 86
Fraser, Simon, 4
Fur Traders, 14

G
George, Chief, 53
Gilley Brothers, 87
Gold Coast, 1
Gold Rush, 11, 14

H
Haida, 51
Hall, Sam, 57-58
Hall's Prairie, 65, 80, 93
Halland, Sweden, Introduction, 34
Halouk, Chief, 53
Halta, Chief, 53
Hazelmere, 54
High-land fling, 18
High-rigger, 85
Hope, 20
Hornby, Robert M., 87

Hotel, Mt. Baker, 32
Huck, 46, 74
Huck, Abraham, 44, 75
Hudson's Bay, 30, 61-64
Hudson's Bay Brigade Trail, 27, 30

I
Huntingdon, 40
Iceland, Epilogue
International Boundary, 40, 59
Ireland, Introduction
Irish Coast, 34
Isinglas, 62

K
Kane, Paul, 1
Kendall, Dr. A. L., 90, Epilogue
Kennedy Trail, 3
King Solomon's Mines, 22
Kinsmen, 27, 53
Klondike, 87
Kwantlen, 53, 64

L
Ladner, 75
Land of the Peace Arch, Introduction
Land Registry, 42
Langley, 7, 16, 54, 73
Letters of Patent, 65
London, England, Forward, 1

Mc
McBain, Frank, 17 >23, 25, 27-28
McClinton, David, Introduction, 35
McClinton, Mary Jane, Introduction
McClinton, Robert, Introduction, 35
McClinton, Sarah, Introduction, 15, 17-18, 20, 35
McDougal, 47-48
McClellan, 37, 42, 73, 86, 93

M

Mana from Heaven, 5
Manager of Heritage Services, Acknowledgements
Meadford, Ontario, 77
Michael, Chief, 53
Mission, 23, 25
Morpheus, 17
Mosquitoes, 9
Mediterranean, 1, 22
Morrison, Sara, Introduction
Mud Bay, 4, 47-48, 69-70
Municipal Hall, Surrey, 75
Murrays' Corners, 7, 11, 13-14, 29, 36
Murray, Mrs. Lucy, 29, 36

N

Nanaimo, 12
Nappenee, Ontario, 16
New Westminster, Introduction, 3, 20, 41-43, 55-56, 58-59, 64, 66, 68, 69, 76, 83, 85-86
New Westminster Southern, 85
Nicomekl, 5 -7, 11, 17, 19, 25, 28-31, 33-34, 44-45, 54, 59, 64-68, 70, 84, 86-87, 90-91
Noah's Ark, 30
Norris, Mary Jane, 73
North Bluff, 51
Northwest, 32, 36
No-see-ums, 10, 12

O

Oliver, John, 89-90
Ontario, Introduction, 77

P

Pacific, 1, 19, 25, 44, 60
Pacific Coast, 1, 36, 40
Pacific Islands, 1
Pallock, Chief, 52
Pearson, John, Dedication, Introduction, Back cover
Pike, Mrs., 69
Point Roberts, 51, 76, 84
Port Kells, 5, 64
Potlatch, 53

R

Robinson, 73
Root-house, 47
Royal Engineers, 63
Royal City Sawmills, 75

S

Sacramento City, 79
Salmon River, 3, 54
Sandwich Islands, 2
Sapperton, 66
Sardis, 23
Scandinavian, Epilogue
School District #36, 74
Schools, 73
Scotland, Introduction, 34
Scott Road, 86
Sema:th, 32
Semiahmoo, 3, 42, 45, 49-52, 54, 69-72, 79, 84
Serpentine River, 3, 76, 80
Seymour Narrows, 62
Shannon, 18, 20, 37, 39, 41-43, 66, 68, 74
Shannon, William (Bill), 18, 37
Shannon, Joe, 74
Shannon, Tom, 18, 20, 37, 39, 47-48, 56, 68
Shortreed's Corners, 33, 36, 40
Sigguurdsen, Epilogue
Silver-thaw, 21
Skeltkalein, Chief, 32
Skous, 48, 51
Slallaham, Chief, 27
Smith, Hurricane, 12
Smokehouse, 28

Solomon King, 22
Sommer, Warren, Acknowledgements
Son of the Highlands, 19
Songhee (Songhees), 53
Sourdough, 14, 16
South Westminster, 12, 71
Spas, Chief, 50
Stewart, John, 89
Stockholm, Introduction, 34
Sumas City, 32
Sumas Lake, 31
Sumas Mountain, 31
Sumas River, 40
Surrey, Acknowledgements, Introduction, 54, 57, 59, 64, 73-74, 78, 86-87,
Surrey Centre, 44, 46, 69, 75, 77, 80, Epilogue
Surrey Municipal (City) Council, Acknowledgements, 68-69, 85
Sweden, Introduction, 37
Sweet, William, Epilogue
Switzerland, 16

T
Techossem, Andrie, 53
Telegraph Trail, 3, 58
Texada Island, 1
Thrift, Henry, (Family), 74
Thompson, Chief Factor, 62
Trapp, T. G., 42
Travois, 39
Trinity College, 75
Tsakawayan Portage, 61
Tynehead, 85

U
United States of America, 40, 54

V
Valley, 14, 22, 39, 58
Valley of the Fraser, (The), Front cover, Forward, Introduction, 1-3, 6, 21, 27, 47, 64, Back cover
Valley of the White Waters, 14
Vancouver, Introduction
Vancouver, Captain George, 51
Victoria, Introduction, 20, 35, 52, 59, 68, 73, 86

W
Wade, Teddy, 80-82
Washington, 40, 54
Walker, J. W., 80
Whattlekainum, Chief, 64
Wells Farm, (Edenbank), Introduction, 15, 16, 35
Wells, Allen Casey, 14-16, 18, 20, 22, 26, 29-30, 35
Wells, Mrs., 23, 29
West Coast, Introduction, 35, 53
White Medicine Woman, 46
White Rock, 74
Winchester rifle, 42-43, 45
Woodward, William, 48
Work, John, 62

Y
Yale, 14, 16, 22
Yale Wagon Road, 30, 63, 86
York, Stove, 12
Yuculta, 62, 64

Z
Zion Lutheran Church, 74